An Incomplete List of My Wishes

AN INCOMPLETE LIST OF MY WISHES

stories by

Jendi Reiter

SUNSHOT PRESS

2017 SUNSHOT BOOK PRIZE™ FOR FICTION

An Incomplete List of My Wishes
© 2017 by Jendi Reiter

Published 2018 by Sunshot Press, an imprint of *New Millennium Writings*.

EDITOR-IN-CHIEF
Alexis Williams Carr

ASSOCIATE PUBLISHER | COVER & BOOK DESIGN
Brent Carr

CONSULTING EDITOR EMERITUS
Don Williams

CONTRIBUTING EDITORS AND SUPPORT
*Laura Still, Rebecca Moody, Linda Parsons,
Chloe Hanson, Joseph Mooradian, and others*

COVER PAINTING
Errancy *by Ariel Freiberg, arielfreiberg.com*

3 5 7 9 10 8 6 4 2

ISBN: 978-1-944977-20-7 **(Paperback)**
ISBN: 978-1-944977-08-5 (Hardback)
ISBN: 978-1-944977-24-5 (eBook)

All rights reserved. Except for brief quotations in critical articles or reviews, no part of this publication may be reproduced, copied, transmitted, or distributed, in any way, without written permission from the publisher. The stories in this collection are works of fiction. Names, characters, businesses, places, events, locales, and incidents are either the products of the author's imagination or used in a fictitious manner. Any resemblance to actual persons, living or dead, or actual events is purely coincidental.

www.sunshots.org
www.musepaper.org
www.newmillenniumwritings.org

SUNSHOT☉PRESS

musepaper.org

For my son, Shane:
Love makes a family

CONTENTS

publication acknowledgments | *viii*

Exodus | 1

Two Natures | 3

An Incomplete List of My Wishes | 27

Today You Are a Man | 37

Waiting for the Train to Fort Devens, June 17, 1943 | 53

Julian's Yearbook | 57

Altitude | 65

Five Assignments and a Mistake | 68

The House of Correction | 80

Memories of the Snow Queen | 103

Taking Down the Pear Tree | 110

ABOUT THE AUTHOR | 141
ALSO BY THE AUTHOR | 142
SUNSHOT PRESS | 146

PUBLICATION ACKNOWLEDGMENTS

"**Exodus**" — published in *Lily*, Issue 5.3 (2011)

"**Two Natures**" — Finalist, 2009 American Fiction Prize, published in *American Fiction* (Fall 2010)

"**An Incomplete List of My Wishes**" — Winner, 2012 James Knudsen Editors' Award, *Bayou Magazine*, published in 2012 issue

"**Today You Are a Man**" — Second Prize, 2010 Iowa Review Awards for Fiction, published in *The Iowa Review* (Winter 2010/11)

"**Waiting for the Train to Fort Devens**" — published in *The Rose & Thorn* Magazine (2009)

"**Julian's Yearbook**" — First Prize in 2008 Chapter One Promotions International Short Story Competition, published in 2012 anthology; Honorable Mention in 2007 E.M. Koeppel Short Fiction Contest from Writecorner Press

"**Altitude**" — Honorable Mention, 2010 Just Desserts Short-Short Fiction Prize, published in *Passages North*, Issue #32.1 (2011)

"Five Assignments and a Mistake" — First Prize, 2011 OSA Enizagam Award for Fiction, published in *Enizagam* (2011); runner-up, 2010 Bridport Prize, published in winners' anthology

"The House of Correction" — Finalist, 2018 Solstice Fiction Prize, published in *Solstice Lit Mag* (Summer 2018)

"Memories of the Snow Queen" — published in *Grimoire*, Issue #4 (2017)

"Taking Down the Pear Tree" — Winner, 2016 New Letters Award for Fiction, published in *New Letters*, Vol. 83 #2&3 (2017)

The story **"Two Natures"** is a prequel to Jendi Reiter's novel by the same name (Saddle Road Press, 2016). Julian, Laura Sue, and Peter are characters from the novel *Two Natures* who also appear in the stories: "Julian's Yearbook," "Today You Are a Man," and "Five Assignments and a Mistake." *Two Natures* won the 2016 Rainbow Award for Best Gay Contemporary Fiction and was a Finalist for the Lascaux Prize for Fiction, the National Indie Excellence Awards, the Book Excellence Awards, and the American Book Fest Best Book Awards.

EXODUS

FLOATING FACEDOWN IN THE POND: A DIARY, BROWN leather stained with mute blue ink. Or a hat, twirling slowly on the water's surface. Pencil stubs, lucky stones; the things in a boy's pocket that sink when dropped. I could make a series of portraits of him from which he would be absent. He is not one boy alone but many, in potato-fed towns and iron cities, at this very moment drawing their last unsuccessful breath. Hear that apologetic gulp of air, feel the thick green waters roll off their final shrug, their well-practiced hands opening to give back everything before it's offered.

Oh yes, there are some whose brains are action paintings formed by bullets, boys whose mother finds them hanging from her discount chandelier, heavy as Daddy's prize fish. But I want to speak of those who tried so hard to be polite, even in death; who, if they could have lived a moment longer after they were hooked out of the river, would have folded their own shrouds as neatly as the name-tagged underwear they packed for Scout camp. Marshmallow ghosts, burnt flecks of campfire ash dancing in the wind you can ignore as you huddle down under your identical blankets. These are the lost boys, the harmless boys, who tore the pages out of their journals and stuffed them in the storm drain, clogging the toilets with their shame. Those wet blue masterpieces of regret, that you try to decipher only now, when the words have been washed away. They are messages you might have sent yourself: *I am sorry for all the pain I caused.*

Remember that hour when you held back the words *Nobody has ever loved me the way I loved him.* I have. I do.

TWO NATURES

WHEN WE CAME DOWN TO BREAKFAST, MAMA WAS burning Uncle Jimmy's birthday card.

"Eew, what's that smell?" Laura Sue squealed, flinging herself into her chair. At the last moment she remembered her manners and settled herself primly with her hands folded on the green-and-white checked tablecloth, anticipating communion with a stack of pancakes. My little sister had been wearing the same blue kerchief every day for the past two weeks of Vacation Bible School, in that sweaty July of 1984, in hopes of being cast as Mary in the end-of-term talent show.

"Good morning, Yentl," I greeted her, and she jabbed me with her elbow, making me spill syrup on the tablecloth. I flung my napkin over the spot. We couldn't let Daddy see anything out of place.

Whatever was in the sink, dampened, refused to burn cleanly. Mama snatched up the half-blackened pieces of paper in a tea towel, dropped paper and towel in the trash, and began scrubbing her hands vigorously under steaming water, but not before I recognized the bright blue envelope with the Savannah postmark that I'd taken out of the mailbox the day before. I ran over to the bin. Mothers have eyes in the back of their head, it's said, and so perhaps do wives, able to see what's behind them better than what's ahead.

"Julian Selkirk, get away from there this instant!"

"But it was my card. I didn't even get to open it yet because my birthday's not until next week and you said —" I would soon be twelve, too old for strategic whining, but Daddy wasn't downstairs yet and Mama was always a sucker for babies of any age.

Not this time, though. She slapped my hand back. "I told you, don't touch that." Mama didn't know how to hit in a way that really hurt, but I pulled away anyhow. "It's got germs on it. You know what kind."

"But it might have had money in it," I complained. It was a feeble protest and I knew it. Uncle Jimmy was the proprietor of a weird little shop that sold orphaned bits of china and used books alongside the occasional stuffed parrot. He lived with Mémère Dupuis in a drafty pink-plastered house she called Beau Rêve. My father's company had just won the contract to build a new 25-lot subdivision in Gwinnett County and Mama had sold an article on low-calorie cocktails to *Southern Living*. The cash flow direction was definitely not from Mama's family to ours, notwithstanding the two months last winter when we lived in Mémère's spare room, which my big brother Carter vigorously pretended didn't happen. Seriously, for the first couple of weeks we were back home, I might say something like "Remember those great French fries we had at the Shrimp Factory," or "That praise band isn't half so good as the choir at Sacred Heart," and Carter would pull a face and say "We've never been to the Shrimp Factory, dumbass," and so on.

Laura Sue looked mournfully at the stack of pancakes, which were turning limp as they cooled. Her hand reached for the plate just as Daddy's footsteps sounded in the hall. "Mama, when are we going to visit Uncle Jimmy?" I asked loudly.

"Hush, we'll talk about that later," she whispered. She pushed an imaginary curl of hair out of her face and smoothed down the front of her rose-printed dress.

"You always say that, but then you never do it," I argued, to distract her. "You've been saying that since he went into the hospital." Out of the corner of my eye, I saw Laura Sue snatch a pancake and stuff it under her loose denim shirt.

"Uncle Jimmy's a faggot," Carter spoke up. He gulped milk out of the cow-shaped creamer so his cup would still look clean. "We saw the video about it in health class."

"Children, watch your language," was all Mama said. She had that pinched, puckered expression on her face like she was shrinking inside, like the house that implodes at the end of *Poltergeist*.

"This guy in the video lost all his hair and he had these big purple sores on him like a leopard," Carter went on.

"Leper, asshole," I said, my voice cracking. And there he was, suddenly. Our Father, who art in the kitchen.

How can I describe Daddy? My mind slides away from picturing him as just another object in the room, on a par with Laura Sue's pinched cheeks and unruly auburn curls, the dull silver curves of the coffee pot, Mama's wide dark eyes carefully framed with mascara and foundation over a yellowing bruise, the pink rounds of Canadian bacon cooling in their grease. I see my brother's face, a rough copy of the big man's, with fleshy forehead and small eyes. But Carter's shoulders are hunched where Daddy's are straight, his hands, still grimy from yesterday's scrimmage, too large for his china cup, while Daddy knows just how to hold a briefcase, a dollar, a bottle, a woman.

"What did you say?" Mild-mannered this morning, on the surface, an ordinary businessman in his pressed white shirt that by day's end would be stained with sweat and enthusiasm for the big score, so many acres bulldozed and walls raised.

"Nothing, sir," I muttered. Carter opened his mouth to tell on me but reconsidered. He'd deal with me later, if he remembered. Wiry and small for my age, I could no more beat my brother in a fistfight than I could resist provoking him, like the time I told him Daddy had named him after his favorite bluegrass band (which was true) and that the real name on his birth certificate was Mother Maybelle (which was not).

Daddy shouldered his way past us to get a cup of coffee. We all prayed it was still hot. I was tired of this routine. In a few days I would be twelve, five or six more years and I could go to college, or travel the world, like Uncle Jimmy before he got sick, finding treasures in the back rooms of shops in Morocco and Shanghai, where Pastor Steve said the heathens lived. Thinking of Uncle Jimmy made my stomach constrict. This was the last birthday card I would ever get from him, I knew that, and it was nothing but a heap of disinfected ashes in the garbage, underneath the eggshells and coffee grounds, like he would be soon, dead and underground, and nobody was willing to say so.

I felt the heat of Daddy standing behind me. He smelled sober, like aftershave and shoe polish, and I hoped he could keep it together until my birthday. Last summer we'd gone camping, and while the girls drank cocoa in the tent and slapped at mosquitoes, Daddy and Carter and I had played at being Indians in the woods, stalking each other and trying not to make any noise when we stumbled on sharp rocks and walked into branches. That's why our baseball team was called the Braves, Daddy said, because Indian warriors were so brave that they didn't let out a sound even under torture. In the starry blackness of the woods, I had felt their massacred ghosts around us, watching, inaudible, unsuspected.

Outside, a car honked — Darcy Preston's mother waiting to carpool us to camp. "Won't you sit down and have some pancakes, Brad?" Mama pleaded to Daddy, calculating that she had about three minutes to get some nutrients into her precious children.

Daddy poured out the rest of his coffee in the sink. "Meeting with the bank at nine," he announced. "Houses don't pay for themselves, y'know." He smiled at his own familiar remark, and we relaxed. Mama glowed as he patted her cheek, the flat of his hand alighting there gently. "Hansons coming for dinner tonight. Wear something decent." And instantly she faded, like a weak winter sunbeam.

Laura Sue and I made a dash for Mrs. Preston's Buick, while Carter hopped on his bike. Having aged out of Bible camp, he was free to play football with his buddies all day. I sat in the front seat while Laura Sue and Darcy pretended to get along in the back. Darcy didn't have to pretend very much because she had long blonde hair and had once been in a pet food commercial with her dog Sal. She still spoke like the cameras were rolling, with that over-enunciated good cheer.

My sister passed me half of her stolen pancake. It was linty but I ate it anyhow. "Mommy, Laura Sue isn't sharing," Darcy complained.

"To them that hath, more shall be given," I retorted. "Bet you don't know which chapter and verse that is."

"What do you want to bet?" she bluffed.

"If you're wrong, you'll cut off all your hair."

"Julian, behave," Mrs. Preston snapped.

"Cutting off your hair is an important spiritual discipline," I argued. "Nuns do it all the time."

Bad move. Mrs. Preston sniffed. I'd forgotten we weren't in Savannah anymore, where Catholics were considered Christian. I had sung a solo in "Laudate Pueri" (probably my last turn as a darling boy soprano) at the Christmas concert at Sacred Heart, while Mémère dabbed her sparkling eyes with a lavender silk handkerchief. I was too young to know the term "liturgy queen," but I couldn't take my eyes off the gangly young deacon who laid out the gleaming chalice and cruets so gracefully on the altar, like Mama setting the table, a table that would stay the same forever.

When Mama fell down the stairs last Thanksgiving, Daddy had taken us kids out for a steak dinner. To cheer us up, he said. He was so solicitous, his big face flushed with wine, re-folding Laura Sue's napkin every time she ran for the bathroom, letting Carter and me order off the menu like real adults. I pushed my privileges to the limit, to see if we could get away with ordering lobster tails and jumbo onion rings for dinner, and when it came I had no intention of eating any of it. Daddy's good cheer grew over-inflated, dangerously close to bursting, each time he would glance up from his plate and see the three of us sitting still, unable to open our mouths.

The following morning Uncle Jimmy had pulled into our driveway in Mémère's 1968 turquoise Thunderbird. He said he was taking us to visit Mama in the hospital, but he left Laura Sue and me down in the lobby gift shop for the longest time while he and Carter went up to her room. When they came back, they were pushing Mama in a wheelchair. They pushed her right out the front doors and lifted her into that boat of a car, stretched out on the back seat with her head on my lap and her plaster-encased legs across Laura Sue's knees, and four hours later we were in Savannah.

Our escape was sudden and unendurably slow, all at once. Every curve on the interstate jolted Mama's slumping head, her hair darkened with sweat across her forehead. I was on mascara duty, dabbing her tears away with a tissue between rest stops, holding up the pocket mirror so she could repair the damage when we pulled over for gas. "I can't let your Mémère see me like this," she moaned, fussing with the sweater Uncle Jimmy had thrown over her hospital gown. Laura Sue hung onto her legs like a drowning person clinging to a spar. Carter got to ride up front and hold the map, which was useless because we already knew where we were going.

I was grateful to Uncle Jimmy for keeping him busy. My brother had been the first to voice what was happening to us, which he did with his usual tact and charm. "If I was going to run away from home, I wouldn't take you with me," he grumbled to me in the parking lot of the Burger King outside Macon. He was stuffing his face with a fruit pie and at that moment I thought I'd never seen such a disgusting sight in my whole life.

"Well then, when we get there, you can just keep on going," I said, and kicked him in the shins. My brother, who had once eaten five raw eggs on a dare without puking, who scored the winning goal in peewee soccer with a bloody hole where his two front teeth used to be, my brother dropped his fruit pie on the asphalt and began to cry.

"I'll come with you," I said. Still the tears streaked his big red face. Because I knew he wouldn't want me to touch him, I scooped up the fruit pie from the pavement.

"Dare you to eat that," he gulped.

I examined the squashed pastry, oozing red jelly dotted with black flecks of gravel. In a way, everything was mashed into everything else, clean and dirty, sense and no sense. Disgusting was just one way to look at it. I flashed back to the time we'd gone camping and Daddy had taught us how to dig a latrine. Now maybe I'd never see him again. I felt like the top of my head was floating away. To stop it, I lifted the fruit pie to my mouth, but Uncle Jimmy intervened.

"Julian, don't be such a *savage*," he scolded, but with a wry smile. "Get in the car, you two, and try not to set each other on fire for the next fifty miles."

TWO NATURES 11

Back in our mobile rescue unit, I watched the back of my uncle's head as he sped calmly down the highway. On past vacations, I'd joined in, somewhat reluctantly, when Carter and Laura Sue made fun of him behind his back, mocking his soft reedy voice, his rooster-like shock of reddish hair, the dusty corduroy blazers he wore in shades of plum and olive green. Did he know? Would it have mattered? Maybe now our lives would be so quiet that we would stop wanting to be bad.

Naturally the arguments started as soon as we settled into Beau Rêve. The three of us over bed space, lights-out time, whose clothes were on which side of the tiny room. Mama against Mémère over what came next. Us against Uncle Jimmy, because we could. *Beautiful dream.* Mémère had named the old pink house after the Louisiana plantation that her father lost when his commodity trades went bad. She had been a high-end milliner in the French Quarter before she married a Georgia man. We used her feathered creations to play Zorro, sliding down the long mahogany banister with terrible war cries, glee tempered with anxiety as the holidays passed and we were not sent to school.

At night, fed up with Laura Sue's whimpering and Carter's snoring, the smelly familiarity of us, I would creep halfway downstairs and sit on the landing. *I am a soldier,* I imagined, *sleeping on the hard, cold ground.* The women's voices drifted up from the parlor. Though I couldn't see them, I knew Mémère was ensconced before the fireplace, drinking Amaretto-laced hot cocoa, perhaps resting one hand on the silver knob of her cane. Mama would be on the sofa, her plain wooden crutches within easy reach. "It's not that simple, Maman. The boys need a man in their life."

"Not that one," Mémère growled.

"Bradford is a *good* father," Mama pleaded. "He gets carried away with discipline sometimes, but I don't know, maybe that's what children need, to grow up strong and — and *proper.*"

In the dark of the landing, I felt the chill of Mémère's silence. Widowed early, she had raised her two children alone in this house, excepting the occasional servant. "Discipline? Your daughter is nine years old and still wets the bed, your older son's a hoodlum, and Julian — well, Julian's the only one who might have potential, if he'd stop sneaking around and say what the devil's on his mind."

My mother choked back a sob. It was wall-to-wall girl tears in the house that night. If she began wetting the bed too, I was going to run away in earnest.

"I'm only trying to do my duty," she protested.

Mémère spat something in French that translated literally as "pigs' testicles." The grandfather clock ticked heavily in the front hall. I wrapped my arms around myself to keep warm. Now I was no longer a soldier, I was one of the violinists on the Titanic, scraping out "Abide With Me" with deliberate slowness as the icy black waves foamed higher, seductive in their immensity.

"Don't drag the children into this," Mémère's voice cut through my reverie. "You've always been crazy in love with that man and no mistake."

My mother sighed, or perhaps it was the wind, the whole creaking house conceding the point. "You don't understand. He really loves me. He always makes sure

I have the best things. I just need to work harder to keep the house under control, because he has a stressful job and deserves to relax when he comes home."

La-di-dah, boring sitcom excuses. I knew what she wanted from him. We weren't supposed to know such things existed, but Carter had found some wrinkled copies of *Playboy* in their closet and shared one with me in exchange for my Boba Fett action figure, a trade I instantly regretted.

Mémère was right, as always. Children change nothing. Even on the soap operas, we're a hindrance, disappearing at infancy and returning two years later from Swiss boarding school as gorgeous, troubled teens. All through that sparkling December and sodden January, our parents were that age again, Daddy lovesick and reckless, ringing us up at all hours, Mama by turns flustered and coy, smiling as the phone jangled unanswered. My brother grew tired of tearing the place apart and spent his evenings in the basement of the house across the square, playing Space Invaders with the son of a woman who sold postcards at the Confederate Museum. Laura Sue took up needlepoint. I rehearsed with the boys' choir at Sacred Heart after finishing the rather eccentric lessons Mémère assigned in lieu of school: learning all the country flags in the *Encyclopedia Britannica*, for instance, or memorizing bits of the *Norton Anthology of Modern Poetry*. Father Louis was a large, stoop-shouldered man who smelled of whiskey and Brylcreme, and had droopy, basset-hound eyes. His steady mournfulness somehow increased for me the appeal of a priestly vocation.

And then, bones mended, Mama announced that we were going home. Laura Sue cried, as if she hadn't cried just as hard when we left Atlanta. She'd become the darling of Mémère's sewing circle, who praised her crookedly stitched napkins and fed her lemon bars. Carter swore undying friendship with the postcard woman's son and spoiled his last good shirt pricking their fingers to be Indian blood brothers. And I took pictures of everyone with the new camera Mémère had given me for Christmas, borrowing madly against my allowance from Mama, who felt guilty enough to buy me film whenever I asked.

Our final night, again unable to sleep, I took up my place on the landing. This time I didn't want to pretend it was anything but itself, the old wooden staircase of Beau Rêve, down which Mama would descend into Daddy's arms tomorrow like it was their wedding day, like when you've watched *Gone With the Wind* all the way to the end and you rewind the tape so you can see Tara as it used to be, green and full of laughter.

The front door opened, painting a streak of light across the floor. In the glow of the streetlights I saw Uncle Jimmy, wrapped in his striped scarf and overcoat, and a young man I didn't recognize. They were both bareheaded despite the cold, and the other man's tousled blond curls shone almost as brightly as his fair skin. As I watched, my uncle put his arms around him and touched his mouth to those gently curved lips. They hung together like that, seeming to breathe one another's breath.

My camera's shutter clicked. At the sound, the two men pulled apart. Uncle Jimmy looked up. The shadow across his face might have been regret, or reproach. It was

TWO NATURES 15

not surprise. The square of light vanished as the door closed behind the golden-haired man. I fled up the stairs, into the deeper darkness, past our room (soon to be ours no longer) and up to the attic. There I pulled the little door shut and leaned against it, panting, under the low eaves. I had done exactly what was expected of me, and that was precious little.

I held my camera away from me, imagining something warm and alive trapped within that nondescript box. The dusty, mildewed air caught in my throat. *You wanted to see, Julian, well, then see.* We were leaving Beau Rêve because I hadn't behaved, any more than the others. Carter was the one who broke Mémère's vase, now lying in shards in a cardboard box up here next to the water-stained dressmaker's dummy, and Laura Sue had spoiled the mattress, it was true, but I could have stopped them, if I knew so much better, if I'd cared. One taste of freedom from Daddy and we all went crazy.

The attic smelled like Sacred Heart, musty and full of interesting secrets. I got the idea into my head that it would all vanish with the sunrise, like Cinderella's dress turning back into sticky cobwebs. Goodbye to the iron-banded trunk, goodbye yellowed stacks of dress patterns, plaster St. Joseph, unshaded lamp. I didn't dare take another picture to remember it by. To see, to see and do nothing, to see what I shouldn't have seen, to break it like a hatching insect's wing, that experiment all schoolchildren ruin.

I rubbed my eyes hard with my fists. My knuckles felt wet. I would *not* cry. Not a sound. My throat was sore with the effort.

Footsteps shook the stairs. I kept my back to the door. In the attic window I saw the reflection of my uncle standing behind me. My shoulders stiffened. I'd never been afraid of him before, silly old Uncle Jimmy with his beaky nose and elbow-patched jacket, but then I'd never given him a reason. Our teasing hadn't scratched his protective coloration, not the way I had, shining a light on that thrilling, unnatural kiss. It was wrong, what he'd done. I would tell him that if he tried to hit me.

But he didn't come any closer. "Are you all right, Julian?" Still I said nothing. "Are you angry?"

This role reversal was so surprising that I nearly turned around. Yes, I decided, I was angry. This place was crazy and everything we'd done here was a waste of time. I clenched my fists.

"I'm sorry we can't keep you here," my uncle said. "It was rather nice, having some life in the old place for a change." He chuckled. Then his voice turned serious. "But Bitsy believes your father deserves another chance, and when the Dupuis women get an idea in their head, there's no prying it out again."

"Mama's stupid," I burst out.

He sighed. "She's in love."

"Then love is stupid."

He came up beside me. I waited for him to try to touch me, but he only stood there, watching the clouds scrub the pale disk of the moon, dim and bright, dim and bright.

"Sometimes," he said, "it's okay to feel stupid. And a lot of other things, too." He offered me his spotted handkerchief.

"I'm not crying."

At this obvious lie, he looked at me sternly for the first time. "You're an unusual person, you know that." It wasn't a question. "You like to understand how things really are. But what are you going to do when you find out?"

"Does Mémère think what you did with that man was wrong?"

His mouth tightened into a thin line, which he attempted to shape into a smile. "Even your almighty grandmother has to realize you can beat a dog all you want, but it's not going to turn into a cat."

"Does that mean I'll *never* be good?" The tears spilled out.

"Oh, Julian." He sighed again. "You'll be good when you want to be good."

At last I crept into his arms. We sat together on the deep window ledge. The stars glittered in the cold air that blew in through the rattling panes. Eventually I must have fallen asleep, because I woke up on the couch in our room, to the sound of Carter throwing his sneakers into a suitcase, and our life speedily rewound itself to where it had begun.

Now, half a year later, Daddy was fine and Mama was acting fine and I was playing an angel in the Vacation Bible School pageant and the summer sun was shining and Uncle Jimmy was going blind. I had seen that same video they showed Carter's science class; even down south they had to talk about it eventually, if only to teach us about the dangers of blood and needles. This was 1984, so we were also afraid of kissing, sharing a spoon, or sitting on the seat of a bus that had been to San Francisco. And that other thing, of course, that the beautiful boys had done to each other before they began tumbling into the orchestra pit, collapsing behind their barber chairs, taking a spill into the bouquets of roses arrayed in their climate-controlled shops. We had always been afraid of that.

At Roswell Street Baptist Church summer camp, however, all was bright and cheerful as we rehearsed our assigned parts with much roughhousing and off-key singing and adjusting of bathrobes, with the exception of Laura Sue who had locked herself in the girls' bathroom because her nemesis, Darcy Preston, had beaten her out for the role of Mary. Pastor Steve's young wife was trying to lure her out with Rice Krispie treats, but like the manna in the desert, these were not enough to boost my sister's flagging faith. Laura Sue had always cared the most about being the perfect one, a china ballerina too sweet to smash. Given the stakes, I could see why she was having a Gloria Swanson moment. I could have told her not to bother, though, since Daddy was generally unimpressed with matters religious. It was something women did, like cleaning the oven — necessary, perhaps, but not interesting.

But I was not around to cajole my sister, because I was wrestling with Bill, who had been assigned the role of Jacob. To prolong the scene, and give us time to remember our lines, we threw in a few chokeholds and smashed each other against the turf in a style more reminiscent of Madison Square Garden than Peniel. He was bigger than me and usually landed on top. Time and again his stout knee bore down on my belly, my face pressed into his sweaty collarbone, our arms gripping and pushing against each other. I let out a winded sigh that stirred his damp black hair. He elbowed my ribs. "Julian — your line!" he whispered.

"Let me go," I mumbled hesitantly, "for the day is breaking."

"I will not let you go unless you bless me!" he shouted.

My mouth opened, empty of words, so close suddenly to his cheerful round face. I felt heat all down my legs, and shivered.

"Ooh, Julian has a boner!" called out one of the girls watching us.

My face flushed red. Shoving a surprised Bill away from me, I pulled myself up. "I don't want to be in this stupid faggot show," I said. Then I ran for the woods, stopping only when the stitch in my side was sharper than the memory of how close I'd been to kissing a boy.

Southerners know all about curses, how they make themselves known by slow inexorable signs, in the dusky complexion of the slaveowner's heir, in the fitful sleep of the madwoman's daughter. Signs for which you checked yourself every day, like residents of a fallout shelter, telling yourself that your teeth were no looser, your hair no thinner.

This is not going to happen to you, Julian, I told myself, resting my face against the rough bark of a tree to remind myself that I was still here, among the saved children of Georgia, and not in the lake of fire reserved for communists, idol-worshippers, and homosexuals. When I thought of my uncle in pain like that, I wanted to scream.

"Well, it looks like the Selkirks have called an actors' strike," drawled Pastor Steve, who had come up beside me unnoticed. Through a gap in the trees I saw Darcy swanning around as Mary looking for her runaway boy, while Donny Jenkins warbled "On My Father's Side" to the synagogue elders. I hung my head and stared at the dirt. Penitence was the quickest way to avoid telling adults what you were thinking.

"Did you and Bill have a fight?"

I shrugged, which wasn't exactly lying.

"Would you like to tell me what happened?"

Again I was speechless before Pastor Steve's warm, puppyish energy, and something else beneath it that stirred up even more hopeless, angry yearnings. *Blessed assurance, Jesus is mine.* "You know, Julian," he said gently, "it's normal for boys your age to have all kinds of confusing feelings. You just need to ask God to help you direct them into channels that are more natural and wholesome." He paused, with an encouraging smile. "Do you understand what I mean?"

I did and I didn't. Who doesn't want to be someone else? That was why my sister was on a hunger strike for the privilege of reciting two lines to a couple of kids with cotton-wool beards. But how to stop what my body was doing was beyond me. *If your right eye offends you, pluck it out.* Sometimes I thought I'd rather be dead than blind, not that God was waiting on my opinion.

"How do I do that?" I asked. My voice sounded alien, cracking into manhood with a few sharp notes, like the stuck keys on Mémère's piano.

Pastor Steve stroked his beardless chin. I sweated and reminded myself to breathe. Would the rest of my life be like this, suppressing a madness that could be set off by a flash of skin, a smile, a careless touch? I wished I could ask Carter if it was just as bad for him, waking up hot in damp sheets, unable to solve for X because the math teacher was wearing a tight sweater. With my father I could only listen to the sounds from the room next to ours, the creaks and thumps and cries that were sometimes of pleasure. Everyone was stuck in this same stupor, and only God decided when it should stop.

"I've noticed that you spend a lot of time alone," Pastor Steve mused. "Taking pictures."

"I'm going to be a photographer when I grow up." At that time I had dreams of exploring South American jungles for *National Geographic*, facing down pygmies and crocodiles.

"You like taking pictures of pretty girls?"

"Sure, I guess." It was better than talking to them.

"Well, maybe you could take the next step and ask one of them out." Mistaking my confusion at this non sequitur for anxiety, he went on. "Come on, don't be shy. You're twelve now, you'll be a teenager before you know it. Time to start thinking about these things."

Back at camp, negotiations were still at a standoff. When she saw me, Darcy flicked her long blonde hair over her shoulder and winked in a most un-Marian way. Remembering Pastor Steve's advice, I twitched one side of my mouth up in a smile. She was so excited that Donny, as young Jesus, had to tug on her arm to remind her that she was supposed to be looking for him. Inside me, a fresh restlessness overlaid the old. This new power of being desired — what was I supposed to do with it?

To quote Spider-Man, or maybe Winston Churchill, with great power comes great responsibility. At the snack break I brought Darcy a frozen orange juice pop and a proposition. "If you swap parts with Laura Sue, I'll take you out to the movies."

She licked the juice pop delicately as a kitten. "I don't know. Are you sure you *really* want to go out with me?"

"Sure I do. I'll see anything you want, even if it's about horses and Shirley MacLaine crying."

She giggled. "I like you, Julian. You're not like other boys. You say the funniest things."

And so I gave Laura Sue her debut as an actress and Darcy's as a fag hag, sitting beside me in the darkness of the Corona Theatre watching Tom Hanks fall in love with Daryl Hannah in *Splash*. Despite myself, I became entranced, not with Darcy's cool little hand in mine, but with the story. I *was* sad-eyed, baby-faced Allen, working alongside his fat, lusty brother Freddie in the fruit warehouse, pining for a magic that no ordinary woman seemed to possess. Then I was Madison, golden-haired and innocently nude, a mermaid lost in the two-footed world, learning English from the TVs at Bloomingdale's while dodging the unexpected splash of water that would expose her. I almost couldn't watch how Allen's face changed, from infatuation to hurt and disgust, when he opened the bathroom door and saw her beautiful guilty face wreathed in steam and that scaly tail arcing out of the tub.

I glanced over at Darcy. Her eyes shone with the big screen's reflected light. She was like me, in love with something we mistook for each other. Believing herself ready to wager it all on that first plunge, until — "I'm in love with a *fish*," Allen laments, unable to face himself, or her.

The next part of the movie was the same as *E.T.* — the escape from the laboratory, the triumph of love over science. Of girls over boys, or boys over men? Back to the ocean she goes. If you love something, set it free. By that standard, no one in our family would ever see each other again.

"People fall in love every day," Allen tells Freddie, his excuse for letting the mermaid leave him behind in his sad, safe life. John Candy, as Freddie: "Well, that's a crock. A lot of people will never be that happy. *I'll* never be that happy!" When a clown yells at you, take it seriously.

So he follows her after all, giving up the last sight of land and the people he knew, to become what he was — a man who could breathe underwater, who loved a fish. I trembled, electric with something I had no words for. Fear, possibly — fear that my body wasn't big enough to contain what I felt. Darcy squeezed my hand. If I was ever going to start liking girls, it would have happened then, when she saw the tears on my face and didn't laugh.

But it wouldn't happen, I knew that as I popped a kiss on her strawberry-scented cheek before her beaming mother let me out of their car in front of my house. The Buick's taillights faded into the trees that were darkening with sunset, ripples of crimson flowing into violet and blue. Somewhere up there was heaven, where I would probably not be going, so I had better take a good look at it now.

Through our picture window, I saw my parents at dinner. Mr. Hanson from the bank was there, and his wife with the Nancy Reagan hairdo. The candle flames flickered. Daddy leaned over to his business partner, Mr. Crosby, and said something that made them both guffaw. Mama stood behind them, gripping the soup ladle tightly, so she could serve without spilling a drop. On nights when there was company we were supposed to eat in the kitchen, but I was full of popcorn and the fear of eternal damnation, so I crept quietly past the dining room and into the den, where my brother was breaking several house rules at once by eating Doritos on the white sofa while watching *Charlie's Angels*. Soon he'd be too old to care whether I tore his comic books or messed up the battle formation of his army men. *Good for you, Carter*, I thought. *I hope you find a girl like Farrah Fawcett and she lets you stick your face in her boobs all day.*

Up in my room, I was afraid again, as night filled the sky over our quiet suburb. Why couldn't I be like Laura Sue, drinking her milk at the kitchen table, with her ankles crossed under her chair? Then I could find a man to hold me and it would be all right. But what if I picked the wrong one, and he beat me, and for the rest of my life I would have to cry and serve him cocktails? I sank down on my knees and buried my face in the bedspread. "God," I whispered, "make me different." But I said it without any conviction, which was another sin.

There was no one else I wanted to be like. No one except Tom Hanks, swimming through the blue paradise where his love belonged. Were mermaids an abomination, like the shellfish in Leviticus? More to the point, they weren't real. I was betting my life on something that didn't exist.

I groped around among the outdated magazines and dirty sneakers in my closet till I found the shoebox of my mementos from Savannah. Carter had the right attitude, I should throw these old things out and not think about last winter anymore. As I lifted the lid, a faint puff of incense sent me back to cold mornings at Sacred Heart, our blended voices squeaking out scales while Father Louis stole a swig from the flask in the pocket of his enormous cassock. There was the stub of the candle I'd carried in the Christmas procession, next to a grinning porcelain monkey from Uncle Jimmy's shop, which had scared me so much that I'd wanted to own it. Underneath those were some cheaply tinted postcards of Jefferson Davis and Robert E. Lee, and my photo of my uncle's kiss.

I held the picture up to the bedside light. Their faces were smooth and young, their eyes were closed. Nothing in the world existed for them, no sickness or punishment, in that moment when their lips met, warm and alive and kind.

I went down the hall to my parents' room, where Mama kept stationery in a white-painted writing desk that she used for her magazine articles. Not knowing the address of Uncle Jimmy's hospital, I addressed the envelope to him at Beau Rêve. Mémère would know what to do.

I took a last look at the photo, to memorize it, and pressed it to my cheek, as I'd seen Laura Sue do with pictures of Corey Hart in *Tiger Beat*, pretending I could feel the golden-haired man's skin against my own. On the back, I wrote "I love you." Then, my heart pounding, I dropped it in the envelope and sealed it up. I was afraid to write my name on it. I thought Uncle Jimmy might prefer it that way. If he was already blind, Mémère would describe it to him, and he would see that kiss again in the darkness, better than any sight in this world or the next.

AN INCOMPLETE
LIST OF MY WISHES

———————

THE BEST FUNERAL I EVER WENT TO WAS WALLACE P. Chandler's. I didn't know him hardly at all, I just went because everyone else was going, and because his death was unexpected it seemed important.

You know how it is, on a warm and buzzing May afternoon, with those bits of tree fluff lazing through the air, and the campus seeming half-empty but tense with last-minute cramming, all those boys and girls discovering where's that library their parents paid for — on that kind of day, especially if you don't really know the dead person, the mildewy cool of the college chapel feels kind of nice, and the sawing of the cello makes you tired, and you start to wonder about things like how Wallace P. Chandler, who was so fat and short that his thighs made you think of elephant-leg umbrella stands, could possibly fit in that coffin. And when you realize how interesting you find all this, you know it's wrong, but it's the only thing you *can* feel, hard as you try.

I can guess why I'm remembering this today, but I wish it would stop until this plane hits the ground in Dallas, where I'll have more than enough to occupy me.

Not hits, no. Glides through the air, a southwest beeline from Boston, bulleting like the football my ex used to throw to our boy Scotty every sunny weekend in our fenced-in backyard in Watertown. The grass never grew back right; the stood-on, skidded-on patches still show.

The stewardess *clip-clops* down the aisle in her fake military jacket and pencil skirt to offer us coffee, tea, orange or tomato juice. If this silver tube of stale air with us packed inside it began to smoke, to dip and lurch, to maybe hesitate for a second on a tilt and then, with a shrug, scream nose-down into one of the fruited plains, there'd be no time to find out our favorite hymns. No time to ask which priest, or whether gardenias were a better choice because Aunt Peggy was allergic to lilies. Some of us on this flight may have made a list like that, tucked into a safe-deposit box, but I haven't. I accept a Styrofoam cup of coffee. I don't see the point of tomato juice. The one time I tried it, it tasted like cold, watery spaghetti sauce. I look around for someone to share this opinion with.

When my ex and I used to fly together, he didn't like to talk. Brian would read the SkyMall catalog cover to cover and then doze off with his finger stuck to the page where he'd fallen for the latest phenomenal golfers' gadget. Brian made things simple for people. He was about golf. Also the Irish part of being Irish Catholic. His co-workers at BayBank were relieved to draw him for Secret Santa. Those traditions didn't catch on much at the college. Dean Hambly, my boss, left a fifty-dollar gift certificate for the Charles Hotel restaurant on my desk every Christmas. The other secretaries and I sometimes traded items women our age are supposed to like: flower-print notecards and scarves, candles in glass jars that smell like cinnamon rolls. Soon as Brian got the place in Arlington Heights with what's-her-name, JoDee or JoAnn, out went every "Old Golfers Never Die" coffee mug and framed photo of the green hills of County So-and-So. I boxed them up really neatly so he wouldn't think I was mad.

Our plane has leveled off at cruising altitude, we're told. What this means is that the grid of towns and fields below is no longer there when I look out the window. Instead we're suspended over a tufted white blanket that reminds me of the fiberfill insides of a stuffed toy. Scotty sure tore up a lot of those in his time, his own and his sister's. Boys break things, I know. Some more than others. The funny part — I thought it was funny back then — was how Holly didn't cry. She loved those stitched-up Frankenstein babies even more than when they were new and whole. I was proud of her when maybe I should have been angry.

Eleven years ago, when Wallace P. Chandler died, Brian and the kids and I were living under one roof and funerals didn't remind me of anything. Dr. Chandler (as we were told to call him) had been the housemaster of one of the residence halls, the one where the theater boys and sad poetry girls tended to pile up. The kind of nineteen-year-old boys who'd wear a bow tie and a velvet jacket, they'd fall all over themselves to get into that dorm. That could explain why the music at the service was so fine it hurt, like sun on glass. The girl's voice spun up and up like she was giving away all her breath and didn't mind.

After that, Dr. Chandler's secretary, Chitra, came up to the pulpit and said the song was from his favorite opera, but I don't remember the name, something Italian of course. Chitra talked for a long stretch about his popularity with the students and his love for rare books and gourmet food — which, I hate to say it, scarcely needed to be mentioned. Her voice was soft and a little hard to understand because of the accent so I found myself once again tuning in and out, waiting for someone to mention what he had died of.

He'd been probably in his mid-fifties, which even then didn't seem old to me. In those days, when an unmarried man died early and nobody said why, you immediately thought of a certain disease. There's not many other reasons to hide. Folks feel good about cancer and heart attacks, maybe not good exactly but *comfortable*, these normal killers that don't need explanation. Say *cancer* (I've told that lie myself) and your listener softens, goes quiet with the memory of a sister's mastectomy, dad's prostate, even a dear old cat's tumors. Whatever makes them feel more like you. You're not forcing them to inquire about anything disgusting — bedroom acts done in a ditch, a face eaten by bears, identified by records of lost baby teeth. Information that makes the listener feel badly paid for her sympathy, resenting you for putting pictures in her head that she'd never have imagined otherwise. Not too different from the pictures that popped into my unwilling mind on that sun-drowsy May afternoon in chapel, wondering whether Wallace P. Chandler had wasted away unusually fast or developed lesions all over his body and if that was the reason for the closed coffin.

I put the airplane headphones in my ears. They come wrapped in plastic to make us think they're clean. They're partway through the movie but it's easy to pick up the story about a young blonde who's got to choose between a bad-boy musician and a sweet but uptight lawyer. I can predict the ending but I don't care. It's simple as cotton candy. A hot energy floods me, *zap*, something like anger so sizzling it's a joy. I'm alive and have no special reason to expect I won't be at midnight tonight, so, like my fellow travelers, I feel free to waste two of the next twenty-four hours watching Cameron Diaz kiss that pretty fellow from the cop show. Living well isn't really the best revenge — it's living stupidly, because you can.

Somewhere down below, on the outskirts of Dallas, Samuel Iseman is ordering his last meal. Mr. Fulton, the warden, will tell me what it was, if I ask. We've had several conversations and he's always been very kind. Maybe he doesn't know yet what he's going to choose. I've read about it some on the computer. They usually ask for steak or lobster, a big slice of pie with vanilla ice cream. A few get sentimental and want meatloaf like their mama used to make. Me, I don't see how you could tuck into a blue plate special, knowing the occasion was that in a couple hours your arms and legs would be strapped to a gurney, and a needle would be stuck under your skin to start the first cold fluid spreading through your veins to paralyze every muscle and then the one that chases it to stop your heart. But I've never known a man who couldn't compartmentalize.

Brian wouldn't make this trip with me to watch Samuel Iseman die. Don't ask me what JoDee-JoAnn was afraid would happen. It's awkward, I guess, for your man to fly across the country with his ex, especially if he hasn't married you yet. But does anyone expect that our eyes will meet in understanding over Iseman's stiffening body, our droopy middle-aged flesh suddenly fit together, united by the miracle of death? If it didn't happen six years ago, during those hollow days and nights without leads, the discovery in the woods, the investigation, the trial — it isn't going to happen now. From the moment the blow fell, we were pulling away from each other, like a graft that doesn't take.

One day that spring when Holly was fourteen, she rode the bus to the mall with her friends Michelle and Deva to pick out some toys and things for a cat Michelle had rescued. Those girls were like that, always feeding strays, picking stranded worms off the pavement, worrying about the planet. One or the other of them would turn vegetarian for a few months every year, till their resolve cracked before a Fourth of July barbecue or Thanksgiving turkey and trimmings, with much gloating by their little brothers. I've gone over this story so many times. It doesn't add anything to retell it to myself now, but I can't help it, as the plane extends its landing gear with a belly rumble. These are the moments when the most accidents happen, takeoff and landing, that slippage between air and ground.

When the girls were in the parking lot waiting for the bus home, Deva wandered off to have a cigarette so Michelle wouldn't give her grief about smoking. She spotted Holly talking to some guy in his car, figured she was giving him directions, because as I said, that's the

AN INCOMPLETE LIST OF MY WISHES

kind of person she was, they all were, even Deva who couldn't resist checking out every man that moved, and later described this one as twentyish, shaved bald, in a blue T-shirt with something like greenish long sleeves under it. Could they have been the tattoos on Samuel Iseman's arms? Yes, they could.

They were convinced at the trial. He didn't speak. There were other crimes, girls from here to down south where they caught him. He kept things of theirs. That's something else men do. They complete collections. As if you had a personal relationship with Ted Williams through that baseball that some of his precious skin cells rubbed off on. Catholics are hoarders, but the last time I believed was the morning I slapped Scotty across the face for sneaking into Holly's old room to play with the china pigs that were lined up on her bookshelf, just the way she'd left them thirteen months before. *Don't you know this room is sacred to your father and me? Sacred!* — I screeched at this little boy, a stranger who stared back from a face gummy with snot and tears. And then I saw that he simply didn't understand that what had happened to Holly was going to happen to him and everyone else. He was still too young to imagine carrying a dead girl's plastic sweater button (that pink one, molded in the shape of a strawberry) in your pocket to pretend she'd be with you forever.

Brian found us taking turns throwing Holly's china pigs against the wall. We'd already ripped down her Sierra Club and *Titanic* posters, all but a couple of torn corners that flecked the plaster like scabs. He bruised me, pulling me away. I cursed him as I hadn't dared at the funeral, when the cousins and the teachers and the priests murmured that he'd been so good, choosing Holly's favorite songs and flowers, finding her first communion rosary to place in the coffin. Not like a man at all. I'd wanted, then, to scream how stupid they were, to think her wishes made any difference.

I don't think death really changes you. Brian and I, that day in Holly's room, we were only finally admitting the kind of people we were. How little we shared.

It's dark now, close to midnight, a hot wind rising that smells like gasoline, the floodlights from the prison yard hazing out the stars. A dozen people are gathered as close to the perimeter as the guards allow. They're holding handmade signs that read "Not in my name" and "Thou shalt not kill." The ones who aren't singing are talking to the woman from the TV news van. Soon enough they'll figure out what I'm doing here. I'm dressed better than them, in my new navy-blue suit and pumps, clearly not part of the same crew as these earnest skinny boys in blue jeans and their cotton-print girlfriends, or the woman my age who's leading the singing, built like a rhino and with a big plain cross around her neck that marks her for a nun. She shakes her head in response to something from a girl with long brown braids, but the girl heads toward me anyhow, her movements light as a ball of fluff on the wind. Her hairdo is a child's, younger than her face, which is young enough, blank with idealism. If she were my daughter — and she could be the right age, fourteen plus six, Holly aged in real-time and returned from the heaven we told her to believe in — if the hands we've all agreed were Samuel Iseman's were tightening

AN INCOMPLETE LIST OF MY WISHES

around her neck, if the choking blackness descended with the knowledge that her raped and battered body would be half-eaten by bugs and animals before anyone found her, would she fight for his life, discounting her own? Looking into her wet brown eyes, I believe she would love to.

We establish who I am. *What do you want from him?* the girl's nasal voice, half quiet plea, half every teenager's complaint to the parent who reminds her what things cost. She must expect me to say *closure* or *revenge* or *healing, justice for my precious child*, or *I just want him to tell me Why*. But the completion I wish for, the disappointment I know is waiting, isn't any of those.

At the reception for Wallace P. Chandler's funeral, they served bacon-wrapped asparagus and Brie baked in some kind of crust and cold champagne in the middle of the day, under a great white tent on the lawn of the college quad. There was a platter of salmon pâté mounded into the actual shape of a fish, and flies were settling on it. Brian at that point had been downsized at Fleet and not picked up by BayBank yet. I used to go to lectures about botany or Russian diplomacy so I could bring home the free cookies in my purse for Scotty. I didn't know what death felt like then, I thought it was about being sad, so I tried to focus on sadness for Wallace P. Chandler and the one meaningful piece of advice he'd ever given me, which was that you should really listen to the other person during an argument instead of just waiting for him to stop talking. And all the time I'm thinking about that salmon and how we'd never have this kind of food at home, but my feet won't budge from their little divot of grass, afraid they don't have the right. It's hot under the tent with the buzz of close-packed conversations and, yes, laughter, static from a radio tuned to violins, and those flies. I pick up a glass of lemonade and watch as a wasp founders in the sticky sweetness, spinning and sinking, knowing nothing but that yellow sugar, until the jittery wings are still.

TODAY YOU ARE A MAN

Superman on batman, the weight of them bound together. Sharp smells of yellow and blue ink, cold aluminum shelving, cardboard dust. Flaking spines repeat *AMAZING AMAZING AMAZING*. Higher up, Will Eisner's thick digests of tenement stories trace his grand-parents' bent backs and Yiddish rants in scrolling lines of brown on white. Green Jell-O alien fingers probe some space-blonde's inflated tits. Peter breathes them in, these particles of floating worlds. Today you are a man. He's so hopeless only a spider can save him, and not the one who told Wilbur's farmer to keep kosher. Bedtime stories from before he was the horse in the Purim play, every year. Bending over in the stockroom, he hoists another box of *SHAZAM!*, his body big but flabby at thirteen. The way he bends over to talk to his father, or rather to listen, one word to Nathan's clever dozen. In a comic book, Nathan would be the red-headed scientist who convinced Congress to build a Mars launch out of rubber bands. He would persuade Steve Trevor to stick around and look pretty though Wonder Woman would never, ever marry him, and by the way, just because she disappears at odd hours and you found star-spangled underwear in the hamper, there's no evidence that she's living a double life. Peter realizes he's too interested in what happens to Steve. He wants to be one of the chosen ones. He works hard and doesn't sit back here all day reading while his boss Jonas smokes another joint at the cash register, his chair tilted back against a wall layered with drawings of dragon fangs and lightning-bolt fists. Laconic, lean Gary Jonas is his father's friend but he acts like Peter will amount to something. Enough to dress him up as the Jolly Green Giant in the Greenwich Village Halloween parade, with Jonas and his friends as the Fruit of the Loom guys. Peter's parents are open-minded, except his mother, but soon she won't count anymore. Three hundred copies of Popeye. Underneath them the good stuff, the wide-eyed, round-assed elfin girls, which Peter doesn't look at. Bending over in the stockroom.

Tears in the noodle soup. Peter's mother winces when she splits open the chicken, its blood-brown organs unsafely contained by cold cracking bones. Five years old, he's at the kitchen table, making tracks in a mound of flour with his Hot Wheels taxi. The yellow paint's still shiny and the doors snap open and shut. It's cleaner than the cab that rushed him to Aunt Doris's when his mother went to the hospital, with huge black vinyl seats that exhaled stale tobacco and pine air freshener when he sank into them. Peter's angry, like God. She'd taken the toy from him during the Shabbat service but he stole it back from her coat pocket when she went to start dinner.

Father still at the office. That coat is the scent of his mother, face powder and fresh bread, that stiff brown wool with the buttons that are shaped like root beer barrels but don't taste like anything. God smashed the Egyptians. He buries his car in the flour. *Never again*, his mother cried when she came home, Peter overhearing on purpose under the bedroom door. His father's voice, deep for a little man, promising they'd try for another baby, but Peter didn't believe it. That was the voice that said when you're older you can have a puppy and a ride on the fire engine. At Aunt Doris's seder he killed the firstborn with grape juice. *We have to thank God for the one we've got*, Peter's mother says all the time now, even when no one else is in the room. Then she kisses his head till his hair feels wet.

Peter knows what a condom looks like. It's a worm, a flattened skin in the gravel by the chicken-wire fence around the Horatio Street playground. Knowing things is good whether or not you can use them. At eleven he solves for x, y, and z. He knows that Reagan is bad but he can't vote. His classmates clapped when he said if Carter lost he would jump out a window. He did and he didn't. The homeless live in the bathroom, though he never sees them. The playground toilets are in a brick hut with green doors that say Men and Women, not Boys and Girls. Since he got too big for the monkey bars, he doesn't know what to do. Cigarette butts under the sink. He wants to study wars. Sixth-grade history is the Middle

Ages, slideshow of lords in velvet and dancing corpses. Zombies in school, who knew? In the bathroom once he saw Walter, he'd swear to it, go into a stall with another pair of sneakers under the door. The great plague of 1348 killed one-third of Europe's population. Walter sits behind him in history and homeroom. He has skinny legs and wears plaid trousers instead of jeans. He brings brown rice and spinach for lunch in a plastic tub. Some of the kids look down at their desks when Mr. Dushane clicks through the slides of Dürer and Bosch, peeled bodies heaped on hell's streets. On Peter's desk, a faded blue ballpoint drawing like a torpedo that he guesses is meant to be the thing between his legs. He spies Walter looking down so he stares at the projector screen till his unblinking eyes burn and water.

Lost, down the drain. Lost on a desert island. A shovel at the beach, red fleck on the outgoing tide. Lost like words in a dream. Like a Latin verb at the chalkboard. Robinson Crusoe lost hope till he saw a bigger man's footprint. Can you be lost and still have company? Lost in a lifeboat, "They Ate Their Young Shipmate," in Hitchcock's book of true-life horrors. The black lady in the subway presses a pamphlet into his hands. *Do you know Jesus?* His father tears it up. *She lost the baby,* Aunt Doris whispers. *Can you remember where you last saw it?* He expects a laugh but gets slapped and cried over. The point of the joke, lost. He's too young to know what belongs on TV and what could really happen. Lost like

TODAY YOU ARE A MAN

a cat on a telephone pole poster. The baby rides the bus through his dreams, now disguised as a bag left under a seat, now a rolled-up umbrella. He pokes his mother all through the Shabbat service. *Here I am.* The chariots of Egypt and their horses. He's got to pee in the bathtub. Green water sucks through the drain, the smiling Cracker Jack sailor tumbles out of the rubber boat, down the rusty hole that goes to gone. He cries for the whole Red Sea.

———————

Once Peter sees a girl in a movie who looks like Walter. He and his mother watch TV late at night when his father's out of town on trial or preparing for a case. Black and white on PBS, the swoop and fanfare of the orchestra, soft-lit faces of women who call their husbands *Mister* Miniver and *Mister* De Winter. The girl wears thick black-rimmed glasses, and when her boyfriend takes them off, she's pretty as a bird. Half the kids in Peter's sixth-grade class use their parents' first names. He started saying *Nathan* and *Barbara* last year but he's going back to Dad and Mom because he can tell she likes that better. Sharing a bowl of popcorn with hot sauce and Bette Davis. When he hits Walter in the face with a snowball his glasses break and a cut swells above his eye. *Faggot,* holler the boys who play basketball with Peter. He's slow but growing tall and the best at blocking shots. They laugh at Walter's scrunched-up face dirty with gravel and snot. "Faggot" in Peter's history book means a bundle of sticks. Flames close around the

bare-breasted witch in the woodcut like the huge petals
of that man-eating flower in *Little Shop of Horrors*.

Sometimes books tell Peter things he doesn't want to
know. Jonas's store is called Rogues' Galaxy. Up front
are locked display cases of strutting, stomping figurines:
Darth Vader in a real cloth cape, Catwoman with
impossibly long legs sleek as black licorice whips. Then
the kiddie distractions, cheap newsprint Archies. In
When the Wind Blows a nice British couple, Mr. and
Missus Pillsbury Doughboy, die of radiation poisoning,
their faces greening like bad cheese in the dim fallout
shelter. On Nathan's bookshelf between *The God That
Failed* and the collected opinions of Thurgood Marshall
there is a slim volume of poetry. Peter's eighth-grade
history class is studying *Brown v. Board of Education*.
Comics and wrestling are the only places he sees what
could be beautiful. At the back of Rogues' Galaxy he steals
minutes, five here, five there, with the naked books. Jonas
strolls past, dusting the shelves, nods at him man to man.
R. Crumb feels all wrong, happy butts bouncing brother
on sister, dog on cat. It can't be that good, to tear through
the picture in his first reader, *Dick Jane Puff Spot*. He's
in Nathan's home office looking for the Marshall book
when he finds it. *Moonflower*, by Ada Porter. The cover is
white with a white lotus, streamlined as a spaceship. Peter
hears words like bells, clean as snow, far-off as stars. Ada
Porter knows prison. Sweet injection. Release into pain.
A client? *Moonflower* is dedicated to "N." In the weeks

ahead Peter will have to study this question, whether separated children can be equal, what separation equals, how equals separate. When he tilts *Moonflower*, a clutch of wallet-sized photos spills from beneath the back flap. A baby, then a girl growing in school pictures year by year, turtlenecks and plastic barrettes and missing teeth, up to this fierce face of nine or ten with dark brows and green eyes like Ada Porter's on the back cover of the only poetry book Peter's father owns.

In the boys' locker room, in the showers. Steam not dense enough to hide who's still chicken-scrawny and who feels a different animal coming on. Peter's black curls have spread to the clefts of his body. He's relieved by basketball's speechless harmony, its intense, shifting pairings. In the room of echoing, sweating green tiles, the boys bellow and flick towels at unlucky legs, chatter too loud to avoid watching each other piss. He's given up on languages, faked his way through *muchas gracias* and *Carthago delenda est,* and is learning his Torah portion by ear. He chose Isaac on Mount Moriah to upset his parents. If he can explain this one, everything else will be easy. Barbara calls it "making aliyah," leaving her job as a social worker for the NYC Administration for Children's Services to live on a kibbutz. The black brushstrokes of the backwards letters are inked into the skin of the scroll. He sees them march behind his eyelids at night. Sounding out the letters on his mother's travel visa. They're calling it a trial separation. Peter dreams of a bound and muscular Isaac straining against the ropes and wakes with his sheets sticky.

————————

When he is born, she isn't. When she is born, he falls off his tricycle and they put three stitches in his lip. When she is born, he's playing astronaut with a casserole dish on his head. He claims the living room for the moon. When he's learning to cut with round-edged scissors, she is screaming in wet diapers. The tricycle hurtles down the asphalt hill of Washington Square Park and he lifts his hands from the handlebars only when he knows it's too late to stop. When she's tying her shoes, he is asking the Four Questions. When he is listening to records (William wants a doll), she is listening to records (me and Bobby McGee), when he is in fourth fifth sixth seventh grade (Brooklyn Heights), she is napping under her desk in Cleveland, sounding out the letters in Buffalo, building a baking-soda volcano in Boston, when her mother is reading to her (the highwayman came riding, riding), his mother is reading to him (Joseph dreamed that his brothers' sheaves all bowed down), when their father is reading to him (I am Spartacus), their father is not reading to her. Why is this night different from all other nights?

————————

The night they take inventory at Rogues' Galaxy, Peter gets lit for the first time. *Let me show you the good stuff.*

Jonas passes him the earliest *Batman,* sleeved in plastic. The joint goes back the other way, damp from mouth to mouth. A thug struck down the Waynes before young Bruce's eyes and the rest is alternate-history. Jonas has a monkey face, comic-sad, thin lips bracketed with lines. *Your dad and I go back a long way.* Longer than Ada? The carton they're sharing sinks under their sitting weight. Thick sweet smoke joins the smell of yellowing paper rising to the rafters. *The cops busted this place back in '75, some short stuff posing as a kid, asking for Fritz the Cat, Japanese stroke books, what have you. Donald Duck and his uncle run around without pants, nobody complains.* Jonas inhales. Peter feels a tropical forest blooming from his lungs. *Yeah, Nathan stood up for me in court. What's the difference between sex and violence? We give 'em Captain fascist America, but show some tail and you go to jail.* Peter giggles. Jonas rhymes again. Batman frowns through his newly constructed mask, which is black, peaked and stretchy, as if cut from a pair of panties that only a mistress would wear.

———————

At fourteen Peter will hoist baskets of grapes and thick ruffled kale under the desert sun. Waking to the whistle of birds and gunfire over the hill.

———————

That you knew all this time.
She was a witness in an old case.

What kind of man leaves his child?
Either way.
That you didn't tell me, when you knew I wanted a baby.
She's not yours.
We could have worked it out.
I chose you didn't I?
You chose everything.
God.
Does she know who you are?
You've been waiting to go there for years so go.
And my son.
He won't last.
What kind of man.
A witness in the case.

———————

There are always wars. And there will always be lemon trees and oil and the nasal wail of old men bobbing their heads in Sabbath chant and stars sharp as glass in the purple sky, but Peter will not always be fourteen and Gilad who is eighteen, old enough to wear a sash of bullets across his chest, will not always lie beside him under the dusty leaves of the olive grove, asleep with his buttons open.

———————

The hamburgers are burnt again. Peter is through with America. Every night dad's burgers with English muffins and ketchup, sometimes spaghetti. Postcards flutter in, sunsets over tiered walls of buttery Jerusalem stone. Ada brings the girl for visits. They put them together in the den but Peter's fed up with TV except for *Knight Rider*. Once an actual letter, three folded pages, and photos of his mother smiling and barefoot among the cabbages. *That couldn't really happen*, the girl says after KITT drives through a flaming wall, and chirps out an explanation about melting points and combustion engines. She wears flannel shirts and her brown hair is unbrushed. He's waiting for his mother to say *come with me*. For school to end. For Ada and his father to emerge from the kitchen where there are no eggs because Peter made a soufflé, just to prove he could, and now he will check whether any of the poet's red lipstick has migrated from her mouth to Nathan's. Wasting his time. The girl is here, after all. Proof of everything. She shovels three portions of the soufflé into her skinny face. Nathan lifts an eyebrow. He's prepared to be amused by whatever he doesn't understand. Day to their night, Barbara claws stones from the soil, gives over on the Sabbath. The thirsty stay thirsty till the day of repentance is through.

Gilad will pin him down sometimes in the barracks and feel how he's grown harder, his American baby fat burned away bending and picking grapes under the coppery sun, fasted away on beans and brown bread passed down the common table, where he will know enough even on the first day to swallow his ache at being seated so far from his mother, all the laughing brown youth together, with him pale as the one peeled potato in the heap.

So no more bubble gum and World Wrestling Federation Smackdown. Okay, kid. Jonas sticks him with books on communism because Peter's hopeful chatter is all kibbutz, counting the weeks of awful leisure till he goes. *Try on Marx for size, big angry bear defending the starving cubs. You like what Engels says about mom and pop?* Peter reads about the bourgeois trap of marriage, sitting on a crate of Archies, holding in the joint's sweet smoke as long as possible, he reads about vows capturing the woman's unpaid labor, licking the orange dust of Doritos from his fingers, another temporary indulgence. All he knows is he's the only one in his house who can fry an egg. *Do you believe that...?* Jonas says he can hold any point of view for two minutes. *Imagine there's no country, I wonder if you can.* They smoke together, a habit now when Rogues' Galaxy goes dark at 10 p.m., and Jonas hums John Lennon. *That's what I'm talking about.* He winks. Peter, like everyone who was in diapers during the summer of love, has grown up with nightmares of the red phone ringing on President Reagan's desk as Russian missiles streak toward New York. *Nothing to kill or die for, the brotherhood of man.* Whether *Das Kapital* is meant for him as a deterrent or a dare, they're the same thing really. Like when Ada's girl Prue is tripping out over Ozzy Osbourne on MTV, playing air guitar like an epileptic, and Peter dares her to try Ozzy's famous

TODAY YOU ARE A MAN

stunt and she follows him down to the fridge and not
only chews off but actually swallows a piece of the raw
rubbery chicken wing, so of course he has to do it too
and they're both sick. Not a bad kid.

At sixteen Peter will be asleep in Tompkins Square Park
and not feel his high-tops being eased off his size-ten feet.
In a cardboard box with a blanket like a sick dog, on the
ground with the manic poets and old men spilling wine
over their beards and those thin white boys only Reagan
could ignore. Peter, invisible, waiting for coins to patter
like rain on the grape leaves of far-off Kiryat Shemona,
slow nights with plenty of time to curse God and start
talking to Him again because you're bored. On the radio,
talk of quarantines, tainted blood, everyone suspicious
of their hairdresser. Nathan won't always win his case
for the wasted-away teacher, dentist, hotel clerk forced
from his job when silence didn't equal enough. Peter,
writing his stories on poverty for the school newspaper,
sitting through verdict after verdict, on the hard back
bench where the old ladies of the jury can't see him. And
Nathan's anxious, understanding look will find his son
across the courtroom and Peter will be glad of one more
thing his father's figured out about him without being told.

God is theirs, birthright more ancient than the ruined
wall that the men fold their prayers into, deeper than

the common well where Peter will hoist a bucket of cool
water for the goats and avoid the lithe dark-eyed girls
who would play Rebecca to his Isaac, encouraged by his
mother's murmurs. God for sure, God possessed for ages
longer than the scrub lands that will have to be retaken
at dawn. Side by side under the olive tree, Gilad will tell
him tales of night patrols through slums packed with
mad men who strap bombs to their chests, children who
beg for candy to lure you onto roadside mines. No one
has seen God but Peter will hear Him marching through
the morning songs of the young warriors who make every
joke and every bullet count. The mothers of the kibbutz
will look for the victory of God in their grandchildren.
But Peter will close his eyes in his dormitory bunk and
see Gilad, slick from their dip in the river, flushed with
homemade wine.

———————————

At fifteen Peter will give up his room to his sister. After
the wedding, when he was gone. Peter will encamp
in the basement apartment of his dad's brownstone,
where upstairs his dad and Ada will open a bottle of
merlot and Prue will play the same folk song for the
tenth time on the used guitar he brought her back from
Israel. Yossi's guitar, Yossi the martyr. Two thousand
years ago at Masada the mothers decided it was better
for their children to stop breathing than to live with the
enemy. Taking away their blue sky and dippers of water,
blessings even a slave could have enjoyed. If they hadn't
all agreed, it wouldn't have worked. Nathan, upstairs,

will be rehearsing his closing to the jury. The case of
the fired fireman. Tuning out Prue singing "Mary of the
Wild Moor" in her flat soprano. *This is the United States
of America. Father, dear father, she cried, Come down and
open the door.* Where a man shouldn't lose his livelihood
for what he does in the privacy of his home. *Or the child
in my arms will perish and die, From the wind that blows
across the wild moor.* Peter in the ganja-heavy dark will
meditate on the green glow of the stars Prue helped him
stick to the basement ceiling. Opening the windows
before she comes. Before sleep, he will imagine he can
hear them above him, each person turning the pages
of their separate books, like the first whispers of snow.

Come see the cliffs at Petra. Gilad and Yossi returning
from a week on duty too jacked to sleep, pulling Peter
from his sweaty bunk, Peter happy to watch the sun rise
over any old pile of rocks if it's where Gilad is going. No
time for Yossi to shave his goat-face or turn in their rifles,
against regulations but the eyes of God can't be open this
early, else Peter couldn't stand so long watching honeyed
light play on Gilad's bare shoulders. Glowing like the
rose-red stones of this ruined city of the Nabateans,
palatial Roman portals nearly flush with the rough rock
face. A lump in his throat with longing for what never
was, a story entered centuries too late, the mountain lair
empty, the hero fallen to bones. Pretending it's sweat
he wipes from his eyes as the others smoke cigarettes
and laugh. A day for ripening olives and tanning skin

under a sun hot as a new-forged shield. The road back dusty and rutted, Yossi's irritating sing-along to the radio jingles for American soda, Gilad laughing with bared teeth then shouting Yossi shouting *halt* the ragged girl from nowhere her scrawny brown arm pulled back to throw and Gilad shoots the child crumples the stone drops from her hand rolling slowly to a stop in the blood-dark sand.

Bending over in the stockroom. *What do you want?* Breathing on his neck. Batman and Robin are silent. He thinks it's a mistake when Jonas doesn't step away. That he didn't hear. *What do you need?* Fingers at his belt. The first step is to shed your skin. Afraid, he gasps, holds still as Han Solo in carbonite. Fingers below. He doesn't understand and he does. What one man can do to another. Superman takes off his gray flannel suit. Cold in the stockroom. He's nothing but skin under his clothes, after all. But torn, but wanting, split, oh full of something hard as metal, boiling roaring ashamed. Hearing the voice in him. *Today, today. This is what you are.*

WAITING FOR THE TRAIN TO FORT DEVENS, JUNE 17, 1943

THIS PHOTOGRAPH WAS TAKEN RIGHT BEFORE FORTY boys turned into soldiers. In fairy tales, transformations are sudden, painless. Seven brothers lift up their white arms in unison and become swans. Forty comical thieves peek out of fat-bellied oil jars. But these forty men waiting for the train to Fort Devens will have a long way to go before they all become the same.

They line up, as for a yearbook portrait, beneath the slatted wooden balcony of the old Bay State Hotel, which must have been a cheap hotel because its front porch is only a dozen feet from the railroad tracks. A place for salesmen and card sharps, or girls who thought they needed to make a quick getaway from their parents' sleepy fireside. Some of these boys might have taken a girl to the Bay State Hotel, after a night of confused carousing, hooked up by an elder brother with a knowing wink that both annoyed and excited them. Some of these boys have never had the opportunity, and are distracting themselves from thoughts of German bullets by imagining the grateful softness of French girls in a farmhouse where a single candle burns in a wine bottle. These boys kissed Mary Sue or Ethel in the back seat at the drive-in and promised to wait for her, and she might have unhooked her bra even though she knew waiting was powerless against male hormones and the U.S. government.

So here they are at the train station, a scene made up entirely of straight lines: the upright men, the long repetitive balcony, horizontals of windows and tracks. Like schoolboys they are still distinct, their motley characters accentuated in a group. Sixty-five years later, is there anyone who could name them all? How quickly accumulation wearies the mind, the way one bird is a pet, twenty a nuisance, fifty a horror pecking at Tippi Hedren in the phone booth. She is remembered, if at all, for that. Some of these boys will drown very stupidly and some will grab desperately at a floating branch that turns out to be their buddy's arm and receive a Silver Star for saving him, that is if his arm is still attached to his body. Some will come home to open a hardware store and run for city council, and no one will know what deaths they saw, because they do not belong to a generation that tells their wives their dreams.

We will have to name them ourselves. The tall one with thick dark hair and a sleepy smile, slouching under the Dawson's Ale sign with one hand in his pocket, like a gambler fingering his dice — that's Charlie, second son, class clown, popular with the best friends of the prettiest girls. He thinks he won't be brave, and he's right. But it doesn't matter what you feel inside, all you need is a good enough grip on the railing when the monsoon hits, says crew-cut Scott, on his left, who deserves to live and won't. Ricky is short, with a nasal voice and big ears, but he knows how to wear a suit. He's used to thrusting his head forward to be heard. He'll open up a bar in Berlin, selling passports to the Communists, girls to the Americans, and every kind of cigarette a soldier desires. Too bad about Scott, he'll tell Douglas, poor dumb Douglas standing at his other side in this photo, who left school in tenth grade and hoped the army would be keener than pumping gas. Doug is big but soft and friendly, at least he is now, which is why Ricky won't at first recognize him after he's killed people.

Handsome Henry, the next in the row, has always looked the same and always will. His face says Sunday School prizewinner, class president, first lieutenant, state representative for Massachusetts. He did what he had to do over there and he really doesn't think about it much at all. Not even when his grandson fires clips of bullets at the screen, making men's heads explode in bursts of digital blood, not even then is Henry likely to picture the plumes of ash and fire that sprung up like black trees seeded by his bomber. It would be nice to tell the story otherwise, but the trains to Fort Devens keep rolling on.

In fact, to understand the war to which they are going, you have to think of trains, those boxcars of bodies that rumble across six decades, into our films and our sleep. The Nazis were great archivists, they understood the horrors of abundance, of over-satiated repetition, how a pile of eyeglasses is the best argument for despair. Sam, on Charlie's other side, is a Jew, though his family chopped some syllables off their name when they moved to this small Massachusetts town. His sergeant will send him through Auschwitz at the end, to round up the stunned and cowering skeletons that are still breathing. Fleeing his people, Sam hides in the commandant's office, as once he hid in the library from the playground bullies, behind the calfskin fortress of the *Encyclopedia Britannica*. Here is other skin, drawers of teeth, packets of hair, sheaves of photos taken of bodies, from bodies. Sam stuffs grandmothers in his pockets, snatches up wallets of baby faces, until the sergeant stops him. Crazy Jew. The tracks to Auschwitz stretch unbombed to the horizon, straight lines in the commandant's ledger. For the rest of his life Sam will collect photographs, including this one: *Waiting for the train to Fort Devens, June 17, 1943.*

JULIAN'S YEARBOOK

DESIRE SMELLS LIKE ACID IN THE DARK. ITS FACE IS A hundred faces, rising out of the stop bath, materializing on grey paper like ghosts. Your ghosts and mine; you knew them too. The football heroes joshing in a group shot, a chorus line of manly awkwardness. There's the clown, the golden boy, the dull and violent sidekick. You've got to remember that snub-nosed blonde with too much school spirit, whose mascara you almost forgot to clean off the backseat of your daddy's car. Memory kisses her lips back to pink, repaints these black-and-white yearbook photos in the streaked denim and poison green we wore when Reagan had his finger on the big red button.

Everything's digital now. Hollywood no longer needs a thousand sweating extras to watch a gladiator die. It's amazing that clients still fly me to Milan or Los Angeles to photograph an actual shoe on someone's foot. I'm a Southern boy so perhaps I romanticize inefficiency. But I miss the days when you put something more than your eyesight at risk for a picture. I wonder how many of us went mad as hatters from the darkness, the fumes, acid seeping under our rubber gloves, the tension of this hurried intimacy with a masterpiece we had only one chance to perfect or spoil.

Pay attention to someone and they'll think you're beautiful. That's the secret behind the camera. I got used to seeing their best smiles, their proudest poses. As long as there was a lens between us, I never lacked friends.

That's me in the Glee Club photo, that skinny boy with the pointed chin and the lock of auburn hair always falling into his eyes. We reveled in hair back then, like lions. I remember the night rides with those guys, packed into a bus on the way to some *a cappella* face-off or to entertain the comatose old dears at the local rest home. We bellowed gross-out jokes, swapped around porno mags (never the type that interested me, alas), then tightened our bow ties and crooned "Sweet Adeline" in four-part harmony.

Diane took that picture, but who snapped us together in the yearbook office, I can't recall. We were the only staff, in a cubbyhole of a room whose one straight wall bore witness to the changing tastes of a succession of photo editors. My contribution to the poster gallery was a black-and-white Cartier-Bresson landscape titled *En Brie*, in which the dark entrance to a long allée of trees towers like a charging locomotive over a bare French field. My big brother said it looked like a giant vagina. I guess he would know.

Good old Diane, my neighbor, my study partner, keeper of secrets. A short and cuddly freckled blonde, she collected pictures of Elle McPherson, on which she gazed with disinterested worship, seemingly unaware of any obligation to measure herself against this ideal. That's how I began to understand fashion. They don't belong to us, those insect goddesses, those long-legged robot queens. Like Whistler's mother, they're arrangements in color, abstractions that deign to take human form so we might learn to forget ourselves. Then the moment passes, and we buy their favorite rings and shoes like relics of vanished saints. It's a living. If I'd been born five hundred years ago, I'd have enjoyed being Pope, one of the wicked ones who sold the knucklebones of St. Edwithius to pay for his pageboy's satin underwear and wound up ass-deep in a lake of fire in Dante's *Inferno*. Instead I work for *Harper's Bazaar*. Diane's still on my gift-subscription list. She divorced early, owns a B&B in Savannah that I've never visited. Too close to home.

She understood what I was about before I did. It never misled her when our mothers expected us to marry. All they knew was we looked nice together, like salt and pepper shakers. I almost didn't go to our senior prom. I'd heard a rumor that some of the meathead jocks were nominating me for prom queen, and the last thing any girl wants is to fight her escort for the tiara. Diane, God help her, always fell for the politicians. Her then-boyfriend sat on the student council, and also, as it turned out, on the student council secretary. So she was all alone in the craziness of June, with her non-refundable pink gown and a coveted makeover appointment at Miss Lila's of Kennesaw. And me, I already owned a tux, and I like to make women happy, temporarily.

I wanted to take Brent Harrison. Everywhere and every way. In 1980s Cobb County, Georgia, two boys' bodies couldn't meet unless there was a naked chick or a football between them. He was blond as He-Man, a wrestler, a sturdy if unstylish Glee Club baritone. Brent.

Mr. Harrison the Third. Isn't that a name that begs to be written in purple ink in a locked diary, maybe with a little heart or daisy over the "i"? Even if he were called Orville McClurkin, I'd do it all again.

We were in this cheap motel off I-75, a busload of tired boys who'd spent spring break singing about talking birds on ladies' bonnets while our classmates were oiling their bodies in the Sunshine State. Mr. Rabideaux had unblocked the Playboy Channel and we were all watching *The Devil in Miss Jones*, which is about a woman and a snake, minus the apple. I stole a glance at Brent across a sea of glassy-eyed faces. He was fidgeting and looking away from the screen, a good sign that he was either gay or born-again. (Not that you can't be both; I have been.) I sat on my hands to hide their shaking. That was around the time Disney released *The Little Mermaid*, another tale of inter-species love. When you have no voice, your life depends on what your eyes can say. I still see the blue of his, as if it were the only color in the room.

Bedrooms are for straight people. I pretended I had to use the toilet. There was a men's room with three stalls down the corridor from the motel lounge. I splashed my face with icy water and thought about praying, decided I was about to go someplace Jesus had never been. This wasn't like bathing with the babysitter. I was a man and I wanted him. Would he come?

He pulled me roughly into the stall, like he'd done this before, with a boy or a girl, I didn't want to know. We slammed against the locked grey metal door, hands and mouths all over each other, desperate and quick.

I thought I'd go blind with pleasure. What a beautiful place it was. I cherished every stained tile.

Fast-forward to summer and there we were, picture-perfect Diane and I, joining the last dance of the Class of 1990. The committee had decorated the hall with tame allusions to Mardi Gras. Sparkling feathered masks hung on the walls, and the centerpieces held champagne glasses filled with confetti and tinsel streamers. In our tuxes and floor-length gowns, it was possible to believe we might grow up, and equally possible that if I stepped outside at the right moment, I would see gas lamps and horse-drawn carriages in place of the row of two-tone station wagons in the parking lot. Boys and girls leaned into each other's soft necks. I envied the hired photographer. It's like I said about fashion. The picture isn't judging you. You'll be happier if you don't try to squeeze yourself into it.

I was the perfect date, neither jealous nor drunk. Diane had some tough moments when her ex spun past with the other girl in his arms. She wanted that movie myth, the night you remember forever, but she's never been able to get the timing right.

"Look at it this way," I said. "You won't end up like someone in a Bruce Springsteen song, stuck in the past because these were the best years of your life."

Diane just sighed and leaned her cute, stiff little pompadour on my shoulder, and we both pretended I was somebody else.

I love to dance, but the slow songs were getting boring. We were going round and round like figures on a music box. When Diane stopped to chatter with her girlfriends, I decided to slip out for some air. I was headed to New

York in the fall, on a scholarship to the Fashion Institute of Technology that I felt both guilty and grateful for. Guilty, because we didn't really need the money, but grateful because Daddy would have packed me off to business school or the Marines if he'd had to spend a dime on me. I was more than ready for liftoff, but that night I needed a last breath of Georgia heat, a final look at the school's stone paths and manicured foliage barely moving in the sluggish breeze.

Something like a cement truck hit me from behind. My face scraped the gravel walkway. Instinctively, I tucked my chin inward to keep my teeth from getting knocked out. In my house, you learned how to fall.

"You like that, faggot? I bet he likes that." A heavy body sat on my back and forced my face into the dirt. I recognized the *haw-haw* laugh — Chaz something, from the wrestling team. Another boy's foot kicked me in the side. I gasped, gritted my teeth and resolved to lie still till they went away. Swimmer's muscles or no, I weighed 140 pounds soaking wet. They could bench-press me with ease. I watched the blood from my nose trace a dark path around the white quartz pebbles.

Against my will, I was flipped over. Chaz's hand yanked my head up by the hair. Before his buddy slammed his fist into my eye, I saw Brent watching us from under the brick archway. I would have died rather than call out to him. Those goddamn blue eyes. Maybe he remembers mine too. Forgiving your enemies is easy. It's your friends that are the real Christian Olympics.

Muttering "faggot" and "queer" a few more times, the boys realized how far they were from the punchbowl and left me lying on the ground. The breeze must have picked up because I felt a chill. I checked for my car keys. Still there. Diane would let us go home now, if I wanted to. As long as I didn't breathe too deeply, I could stand up. In the men's room, I mopped myself up as best I could with wet paper towels. One eye was nearly swollen shut, but at least my nose wasn't broken, and my tux wasn't torn in any really embarrassing places. A new shirt was definitely in the budget.

Stars fell from the ceiling, dusting the dancers' shoulders with a dandruff of confetti. This was the last special dance, just before the crowning of the prom king and queen. The ice-sculpture eagle's wings dripped onto a silver tray. The lights dimmed and the DJ struck up "Tonight I Celebrate My Love." Diane looked lost. I made my way over to her, wincing when anyone brushed against my ribs.

"Oh my God, Julian, what happened to you?" She reached up to touch my swollen face, then thought better of it. A sensible girl.

"I did it, Adrian — I went ten rounds with Apollo Creed!" I said.

"Are you going to tell anyone?" she asked, already knowing the answer. "You can't let them get away with this."

"There's no secrets here, Diane. We've all known each other too long. There's just things we don't bother talking about."

And we paced slowly through that last dance, gliding in and out of the spotlight. Every now and then she closed her eyes and smiled. Someone unsurprising took home the sash and tiara, and the night was over.

Diane dropped me off and left my car in her garage to retrieve the next day when I could see out of my left eye again. As I limped through our front hallway, my mother called out to me from the parlor. She was lying on the sofa with a brandy-soaked handkerchief on her forehead to relieve her migraines. I never heard of that working but she did like the smell. She was still wearing her twinset and high heels at one in the morning. That was Bitsy all over.

My mother slowly opened her long-lashed eyes and took in my shiner, my ripped and bloodstained shirt, the way I stood slightly off-center, one arm tight against my side. "Did you have a nice time, dear?"

I winked with my good eye. "You know what Daddy says. It isn't a successful party unless you need stitches afterward."

Maybe she'd repeat this to him in the morning, and maybe the old bastard would be proud. I fell asleep in the bathtub before I felt the water get cold.

ALTITUDE

The highest point in Pennsylvania is the lowest point in Colorado. Alice had read this on one of the maps Sam had tacked up to decorate his office at the Speedy Garage. The walls' faded mustard paint job was nearly hidden under bumpy pale pink and green relief maps, annotated maps of states other than their own, and archaic town maps with long-lost structures delineated in copper-plate script: railroad bridge, dairy farm, lunatic hospital.

Alice used to think the maps meant Sam appreciated planning as much as she did, that he understood the expectations invested in ivory notecards and tasting menus, their notarized claim on the future. But maps were also what you saw in real time when you flew above the land, west to east, so high that there were no people visible on the checkerboard of suburbs and cornfields as rust-colored cliffs gave way to slate hills and green valleys. *I've fallen in love,* he said, once at the beginning and once at the end. There were many times in the middle, as well, or Alice wouldn't have traveled so far down the road of Hawaiian tickets and cake toppers, pew ribbons and arguments with the DJ, but it was the first and last times that mattered, as always. *You can fall a lot farther in Colorado,* she'd wanted to say. *We're next door to the Grand Canyon.*

But Sam knew everything she could have said. He'd grown up in this town with one gas station, where the trees were dusty blue pines clinging to crags overhead, dry as Martian canals. In Pennsylvania, so Alice and many other people had read, there were coal mines and the Liberty Bell. The hills were low as boot heels and the river wound through them like spilled mercury. It was cold there in the winter, cold as a broken thermometer.

That one time when she was so sick, he had wrapped her in the blankets from the back of his Dodge pickup and rubbed her feet and sung her the only songs he knew, songs they play in bars, like the Johnny Cash one about the auto worker who steals a car one piece at a time. He had made her tea with whiskey and blown on her hands. But he didn't say *love* until the week after, when she'd stopped sneezing.

They were in the Dodge watching the stars come out at the top of a hill on a closed road. But he didn't say he loved her, he said he was *in love*. Alice should have asked, *Is being in love like being in Colorado?* The air smelled like pine needles and cold iron. Soon they could see a hundred stars scattered like the dots that stand in for exits on a highway map. Sam had a star chart in his office at the garage. The Greeks, Alice knew that much, had drawn lines between the stars and called them Orion, the Twins, or the Crab. People memorized this as if it were knowledge. Drawing a line between two points and putting a face on it.

Marriage. That was the logical next step so they almost took it. Alice shouldn't have ordered the hydrangeas. She should have decorated the chapel with red rocks.

The bridesmaids' sashes were too golden, their gowns too green. All that coolness making him thirsty. They should have booked dinner in a cave. At the rehearsal dinner the seven of them clinked glasses on the wooden terrace of the Overlook Brewery as the sun fell forever between fiery peaks and Sam got dizzy. She could feel it, in the squint in his eyes as his father's second wife *hee-hawed* into her champagne. He wasn't ready for this much altitude. The Jordan almonds in white cardboard boxes with their names in gold script couldn't hold him down. All of it would have to be returned. No one ate Jordan almonds anyhow. The vendor would pop them into new packets, smooth as a doll-baby ready for wrapping at the factory. Alice could get on with her phone calls to the baker, the airline, the man who trained doves. *He's fallen in love,* she would explain. And the woman at the flower shop would say, *That's what everyone tells me.*

FIVE ASSIGNMENTS
AND A MISTAKE

The day begins with a dead baby. Not a cherub floating on the ceiling, not a golden head laid to rest on a watercolor pillow, tiny bereaved boots lined up beside the four-poster like good soldiers. This head is dark, is nappy and bloodied, and can't be seen.

The child today isn't dead, it needs to be taken from its mother, and Laura Sue's assignment is to watch. She swings her slender legs over the edge of the dorm-room bunk bed, her feet finding the ladder before her eyes are fully open. Her roommate below snuffles in her sleep, an open chemistry textbook splayed on her chest. Before coming up north for college, Laura Sue was afraid of what she read in *National Review* about immodest goings-on in student residences, but she's never been sexually harassed by lesbian hockey players and only rarely awakens to the grunting of a boy in Karen's bunk. She and Karen are neither enemies nor friends. Laura Sue is cultivating a reputation for being a good listener. Yesterday she listened to Karen doing her weekly purge after all-you-can-eat-wings night at the dining hall. She feels they're becoming closer. Even in New York, people are predictable.

It's some kind of Awareness Week on campus. There are banners strung in a circle in the student lounge, their hand-painted messages facing inward, the placard explains, so as not to trigger traumatic memories in passers-by. To read them, one has to enter the white-tented space. Laura Sue's boyfriend has been to Africa, and this display reminds her of a photo he showed her, a bed shrouded in mosquito netting around a child with grayish-black skin. She doesn't go in.

Laura Sue is majoring in psychology. She's always planned to get her social work degree after she graduates, which will finally happen this spring, but somehow she hasn't made arrangements for September. When pressed, she tells her advisors that she wants to see the world. They approve.

This semester she's interning for course credit in the clinical program. She learns protocols for what happens when a man hits a woman. What to do when a teen runaway is hallucinating in the backseat of your car. When someone bleeds on you. Bites. Jumps. She rides in the passenger seat of police cars. The last time she did that, she was six years old and couldn't stop crying even after the fat lady cop gave her a lollipop. The cop's partner was questioning Daddy next to the overturned grill where blackened hot dogs grew cold in the grass. Laura Sue remembers sobbing with artificial lime-flavored spit drooling green down her chin. Mama was inside with the EMT bandaging her arms so Laura Sue had to scold herself for getting her new dress dirty. The skinny young male cop looked fed-up and tired like Mama did when Laura Sue's brothers acted up. He didn't take Daddy away but instead offered her a ride. The hot night wind of Atlanta summer dried her sticky tears. At first she pretended she was the cop's new partner and they were racing to catch the bad guys, but that was too scary, so she decided she was a criminal, being carried off to solitary confinement.

Laura Sue rides shotgun today with Marge Klein, from the city's child protection department. Klein's compact Honda is a rattling dice box of empty soda cups, cigarette packs, and spilling file folders that shift from side to side as the car rounds each corner. Klein's frizzy dark hair is turning white in front, wisps escaping from her alligator clip.

The child is a boy. He was burned. The mother's yellowed skin means crack, Klein explains. Laura Sue is still learning to read shades of brown: the pucker of a scar, the wet asphalt sheen of a detox sweat. The boy, about five, wails at being pulled away from the TV where the sounds of gunshots and screeching tires are turned up loud. He's wearing a man-sized shiny red basketball shirt that hangs to his knees like a dress, and new sneakers, white as breath mints. Laura Sue is grateful that she feels absolutely no urge to clutch him to her chest and run down the stairs, like a football player bent on a touchdown, like a soldier with a live grenade.

The day begins with dark hands. Laura Sue's legs sweat with the blanket bunched between them. In her sleep, alone, she can lift off again into the *oh* of discovery: how the buzzing in her limbs subsided, for the first time ever, and she was vast and peaceful as a sheet. She was wind. She could lie on the ocean and nothing would stir.

The university is forcing Laura Sue to write about her feelings on Tuesday and Thursday mornings. They believe that social workers need introspection and good grammar. Laura Sue, at breakfast, scrutinizes the cartoon rooster on her single-serving box of cornflakes, mining for a safe source of inspiration. Last week she had to write a page imagining the secret life of a schoolbus driver. The expectations were obvious. Laura Sue's driver restored old furniture. He didn't pull down fourth-graders' shorts or dance in a tutu for college students to laugh at. She got a B-minus. Her descriptions were well-written but, the teacher wrote, *Why would this be a secret?* Laura Sue pictures fine strong fingers rubbing cherrywood, sanding away scars, making wobbly feet stand firm.

As she spoons up her cereal, Laura Sue sees a girl sit down at the other end of the dining hall table. She's wearing a pink T-shirt that says *I had an abortion.* It's not the only one Laura Sue has spotted on campus this week. Planned Parenthood was handing them out, from a stack neatly folded in a cardboard crate, at the student activities fair. The girl doesn't make eye contact, concentrating on her onion bagel and her copy of *Billy Budd.* Laura Sue thinks about Johnny Cash singing *I shot a man in Reno, just to watch him die,* and how you can't be sure whether he's confessing, or bragging, or holding up the flat statement like a mirror for you to say *Yes,* seeing the awful normalcy you share.

Laura Sue's boyfriend thinks she's a virgin because she doesn't wear makeup. They grope sometimes in her dorm room with the door cracked open, as if anyone would stop them. The rule when her Mama was in school was that a lady keeps one foot on the floor at all times. This doesn't really work when you have the top bunk. Tad explores her nipples in cautious increments, as if they're the controls of an alien rocketship. His long freckled face looks pained when they get close to the place they've agreed to stop. He let go once in his pants and acted cross with her. Just for a moment, but it set off a ringing deep inside her, like the sound of a knife on a plate. Between open-mouthed kisses, they make eager plans for their mission trip to Uganda after they graduate. He thinks she will miss showers, movies, her family, and other white people, but she says she won't.

The lesson today is similes. The creative writing students scribble a title across their page, and then are directed to fill the space below with comparisons to describe the theme they ignorantly selected. Love is a battlefield, a rose, a box of sugar. Explain. Laura Sue was afraid of having too few words and now she has too many. *It's like losing your gun at kindergarten. It's like dead birds in your knapsack.* But in the end she can't say what it means. She leaves the piece untitled, knowing she'll be marked down.

———————

The day begins flooded. Rain spatters Laura Sue's nylons and squelches inside her low-heeled brown pumps as she hurries to church. God is like a bus, slow and unpredictable, but once you're inside its big warm space, you forget how long you had to wait.

The gospel choir shakes and shimmers in brick-red robes with gold trim. Their voices span impossible octaves from earthy depths to joyful wailing. When Laura Sue sings, she feels the week's sharp thoughts and unkindnesses rising up out of her mouth like soap bubbles, poor little malformed angels, released to evaporate before God's forgiving eyes.

At social hour she talks to Burt about his new job at the hospital and admires Gloria's pictures of her grandson. She avoids Lorna and Rose, a couple of beauticians around her age who like to gossip, but she overhears them behind her at the coffee urn. ...*Dumped her for that no-ass blonde, like a sister isn't good enough for him.* Lorna, the nicer one, looks back at Laura Sue with an *oops* half-smile, as if to assure her that they don't suspect *her* of being a man-stealing white girl.

Laura Sue became a thief when she was five. Mama would take her on an errand to the drugstore and she would climb and tumble, how cute, spilling the pretty colored tubes of lipstick that would roll into corners too fast to be counted before she scooped one into her pocket. She kept them in a tub of crayons under her bed. Her secret store. One day she caught her brother Julian, who was seven, trying them on at the bathroom mirror. His face was Mama's, the same russet hair and pointed chin, with his thin lips drawn perfectly in tea-rose pink. Carter, the oldest, would have smeared his mouth like a fat kid raiding the jam jar. He stayed away from them as much as he could, playing hockey in the winter, baseball in summer.

Don't use those! she yelled at Julian, but quietly, Laura Sue corrects her memory, because they always had to be quiet. She couldn't have yelled, she must have whispered, an airless fury like cries mouthed in a dream. *We have to sell them.*

For what?

To buy our own house. You and me.

Julian lives in New York now too, in Chelsea, and takes pictures for *Glamour*. She sees him, but not with his friends, who wear tight shirts and talk fast with too much emotion. He went to church with her sometimes when his roommate was dying, but not any more.

Laura Sue is slowly making herself prettier for Tad. She had her hair cut short and styled, and at the thrift store she found a locket on a real gold chain that she wears almost every day. This convinces Julian that she's happy. They go shopping at Macy's for a linen dress for her graduation party, when the rest of the family will come up from Atlanta and she will make an announcement. Laura Sue feels like she's swallowed a glassful of ice cubes.

When Daddy stumbled into their bathroom, holding a damp washcloth to his forehead, and saw her and Julian squeezed side by side on the step-stool before the mirror, outlining each other's lips in waxy pink, he shot out his big arm and knocked her brother to the floor. Mama nailed her, crying, as the only one possible, the good girl who went on errands without a fuss. She was too young to write her punishment a hundred times. Driven to the store, she handed back the unused tubes and wet her pants; the man behind the counter was kind. Julian said it wasn't so bad when Daddy mashed the lipstick into his mouth and pinched his nose and he had to swallow, it was like bubble gum, everyone swallows that. There were worse things than what she'd done.

The day begins without candles. Sara Grace has no birthday. Laura Sue must guess at a date to count from. She hasn't settled on one, in three and a half years. Autumn is so busy. No day presents itself to outweigh this one, and so each May she remembers it more intensely than the other times when it is always with her, like the poor whose paperwork splits the sides of Klein's briefcase.

Another ride-along today, a home visit to the hopeful foster parents of eighteen-month-old Shequan. Laura Sue sits with her knees together on their tight blue sofa cushions and takes in their view of the 59th Street Bridge, its sooty rattling muffled at this height, while Klein goes down her checklist of questions about marital strife and the proper storage of household cleansers. They test the childproof latches on the oak cabinets. The wife has made iced tea that Laura Sue would really like to drink, but Klein doesn't, so she resists picking up the sparkling cold glass.

At the McDonald's where their car is parked, half a mile downtown, Klein buys a Happy Meal. Laura Sue isn't hungry. The tiny commando action figure floats in his plastic sac stamped with manufacturer's warnings.

She remembers nausea four years ago, set off by the smells of others' meals, the swallowed acid of secrets. She remarks on the foster couple's lovely home, but Klein shakes her head: *They want to change his name. Even that young, a boy knows who he is.*

Laura Sue has no head for biology. Karen, the premed, brains rats by whacking them against a lab bench. Laura Sue is grateful there are other people willing to do that. She couldn't look into a yeasty-smelling petri dish and tell you what the cells felt when they pulled apart, at what point the microscopic pulsing exchange of chromosomes became someone who would have been named Sara Grace if her mother had let her live beyond twelve weeks.

Eighteen in her father's house with a baby and no college. This hadn't happened to her. Sara Grace was not born with skin the color of Andy's palms, rose-beige and cedar-scented. Daddy never smashed the doors of the china cabinet, yelling *nigger-lover,* while Mama, not making eye contact, knelt down in her Sunday stockings to gather up the pieces. The furniture repair store where Andy worked for his uncle was still standing but Andy (she supposed) had completed vocational school and moved away, without brain damage from four white fists as he turned his back to the street to lower the store's gate at dusk; and someone had long ago swept up the soft pile of wood shavings in the back room where a boy and a girl had sweated with joy and terror.

Klein says, *Why marriage?* She's upset now that Laura Sue has confessed her plans to put off graduate school. Klein's bought her a strawberry shake, saying she feels wrong eating alone. *You good college girls all kill yourselves.* Laura Sue doesn't binge, purge, smoke, drink, or cut herself. She's engaged to Tad but has refused the ring till she tells her parents. After that, she won't be someplace she can wear diamonds.

Klein says, *Why not you?*

The day begins in heat. Styling irons sizzle in dorm bathrooms; powder and foundation wage a discreet struggle against oily pores. Sunshine weighs down the mortarboards of the graduates, immobile in rows of folding chairs, like columns holding up the roof of a vanished Parthenon.

Later, Laura Sue, sheathed in floral yellow, is taken out to brunch at Knickerbocker, a genteel pub with wood-paneled walls and upholstered chairs arranged too close together around white-skirted tables. She reserved for all of them, but Carter's kids got fussy and his wife took them back to the hotel. If they were here now, they'd be throwing bread pellets and shooting aliens with their forks, Carter morosely wishing to take a swipe at them with his big soft hand and everyone knowing he wouldn't.

Mama babbles happily about the solitaire diamond making its maiden voyage on Laura Sue's finger, the other ceremony old history after two hours, upstaged by a hundred delightful future decisions about cakes, pew ribbons, and string quartets. Daddy's chest is puffed out, his arms draped across the backs of adjacent chairs, as if he's the only man in the restaurant whose daughter has graduated. Laura Sue sees other families packed into the vestibule, getting bad news from the bartender about the wait for a table without reservations. The high-heeled shoes that Julian picked out for her are pinching her feet.

Carter takes a pull at his beer, complains loudly to the waitress that his burger isn't pink enough. *Does he expect her to take it back to the kitchen in her time machine and uncook it?* Laura Sue wonders, covering her smile with her napkin. She would like to share this joke with Julian, but Julian is quiet. He's the only one who's mastered Mama's lesson that if you can't say anything nice, don't say anything. That's why she tells him things before the others. Like four years ago when he took her to the clinic and she told him to never mention it again and he hasn't. He's eating his salad politely like a television actress who's just lost her sixteenth Emmy nomination.

He was so good at some things, her brother, the nuances of heel and toe, matching shade to shade, that she'd expected him to understand the rules, to realize she hadn't chosen them and couldn't be blamed. It was like not wearing flippers to the opera. Like not walking alone at night in a short skirt. When she says his new roommate can't come to her wedding, his eyes darken and the smile fades from his lips, pressed together in a thin line. *And how long are you going to be with this one?* she wants to bite back against the protest he doesn't speak. Instead they ride the escalator down to the Macy's shoe department.

Mimosas are making the rounds of the brunch table. Mama is asking, again, about the program that will be sending Tad and Laura Sue to Uganda: Will it be dangerous? Does she have enough sunblock? Daddy cracks a joke about the missionary position and her brothers, both of them, are laughing. Mama pauses mid-flutter to make an offended face, as if her age is no barrier to virginal pretense, as if the three of them sitting round the table aren't living proof otherwise. Laura Sue sees their mouths opening, their jaws moving in conversation she can't hear because of the rushing in her ears.

The restaurant crowd is drinking up all the air. Laura Sue wonders how she will stand Africa. She should use the bathroom while she still can. The single-stall ladies' room, pink-tiled, with a cloying scent of dispenser soap, is tucked into a rear corridor across from the kitchen. At the end opposite the dining room, a white rectangle of daylight surprises her, an open back door where men in stained white aprons carry swinging buckets to the dumpster.

Inside the bathroom the heat is worse but the quiet is better. Laura Sue's ankles tremble. The new shoes feel like ice skates, barely balanced on an edge. In the mirror she looks exactly like the girl she expected to be. It's not because of anything she sees there that she works the ring over her heat-swollen finger joints and, standing on tiptoe, places it on the top shelf where the extra boxes of paper towels are stacked. She has no plan beyond feeling the sidewalk burn through her stocking feet like desert sand, as she watches the workers at the back door, waiting for the moment when no one will see her.

THE HOUSE OF CORRECTION

"I AM GOING TO THIS WEDDING," ZEBATINSKY DECLARED to Carla. His middling daughter. *Middle.* But the switched word lodged in his brain, as happened more and more these days, branching out tendrils of other words, a not-unpleasant process until he was obliged to backtrack its meanderings to the conversation he'd left hanging. Carla in the muddle, middle-born between fiery David, now a banker in Hong Kong, and beautiful Natalie, who'd played piano in Carnegie Hall, found a husband, and died. Carla taught high school physics and nutrition at Bronx Science. She thought she knew everything about his prions. Or was that muons? He'd forgotten which were the particles that glued up your synapses, and which ones bombarded you without sensation, like a hand passing through a slide projection.

"How, Poppy? I can't let you fly to Miami all by yourself. What if you get confused?"

Zebatinsky bit back a flippant remark. Getting confused in his own little apartment on West End Avenue and 94th, among the softly creaking shelves of books from thirty-five years of teaching Russian literature, was not only harmless but his privilege, his birthright, which middle-aged Carla was itching to trick him out of, with her sly talk of golf courses and assisted living centers in Connecticut. On the other hand, getting confused in a too-loud, too-bright airport that stank of sweet coffee and porta-potty deodorizer was not an adventure he cared to repeat.

"You'll come with me. See, it says 'Isaac Zebatinsky *and guest.*'" He pointed to the handwritten address on the square ivory envelope, the words scrunching together toward the end as if the writer had miscalculated the size of the small paper. "It's a weekend. You can do your lesson plans on the plane."

Carla blinked hard, her way ever since childhood of disguising a sudden hurt. See, he was still sharp enough to notice the important things. A mixed blessing because awareness included guilt for his unintentional dig. She didn't want to tell old Poppy why she was single in her forties but it must bother her more than she let on. Perhaps that excused the tone of her question: "How do you know the Abramoffs, anyway? I don't remember them."

He sighed, buying himself some time with the implication of a long and emotional story to come, as he studied the invitation's embossed sea-blue script: *Rabbi and Mrs. Gershom Abramoff welcome you to celebrate the marriage of his daughter Sarah Nicole Abramoff to Jasper Michael Shapiro on Saturday, February 23rd, at 6:30 PM, Temple Shaarei Tefilah,* followed by an address in Miami. The truth was, Zebatinsky had no idea who these people were. The xeroxed insert with driving and parking instructions held no landmarks to jog his memory. But was his aging brain the only one that mixed up the places he'd been and the scenes everyone knows from dreams or books? If he could call up a picture of his younger self driving down this "Coral Boulevard" (sun shearing his windshield, palms looming above) to visit his friends the Abramoffs at "Temple Shaarei Tefilah" (boxy white cement with slit windows, abstract stained glass, funereal air-conditioning), would that prove it was real?

"Natalie's friend," he decided. "They bunked together at music camp. She used to sing while Beanie played piano." The old nickname for his daughter came unbidden, along with a sharp image of the tatty wool cap the little girl had demanded to wear every day when she was six or seven.

His living daughter laid her hand over his like a blanket. "It's sweet of them to stay in touch. I guess we'll go."

Zebatinsky managed a faint smile. Having won the battle, he began to fear the war. What would happen when they showed up at this big party, if he still didn't remember Rabbi Gershom et cetera? He reassured himself that they must have had a good reason to invite him. And anyway, no one really talks or listens at parties anymore — he warmed to the distraction of an old grievance — what with the loud music these kids play and the tedious parade of toasts by the bride's cousin's best friends.

More important was the strategic strike against Carla's stealth campaign to immure her dotty Poppy in a suburban rest home where two shelves of supermarket thrillers was considered a "library." He imagined the deaths she feared for him: setting his sleeve on fire on the gas range, breaking a hip in the bathtub. His ancestors in

THE HOUSE OF CORRECTION   83

Siberia had risked their lives for freedom, why shouldn't he? At least he'd drown in *warm* water.

Two weeks prior, Rabbi Abramoff had been stamping out paperwork in his office on the temple's second floor, craning his neck toward the picture window for glimpses of blue in January's monsoon skies. In-box/out-box, a comfortable fatigue, an ordinary day. Starred plaques on the pastel walls kept time with his years, proof of funds raised and spent, buildings dedicated, knowledge absorbed and tested and submerged again beneath the information useful for today.

What had made him think of Izzy? Not even a thought but a twinge, as on waking from a vanishing dream of standing at the *bimah* naked. But because the sky looked likely to wash out his lunch break and the fourth-quarter report from the capital campaign was tedious, Rabbi Gershom for once allowed memory to lead him backward.

Maybe it was the line item for the school that had started this. Temple Shaarei Tefilah's day school had little in common with the Lower East Side yeshiva where he and Izzy had stuck contraband bubblegum under their bolted-down wooden desks. Named for a donor who had invented some kind of microsurgical apparatus, the Miami school had computers, peanut-free kosher lunches, and field trips to the oceanography lab. The yeshiva wedged between historic tenements on Hester Street was named Beit Tzedek, the Home of the Righteous, which young Geri re-translated in jest as the House of the Correct, a/k/a the House of Correction. Prisoners they seemed to themselves, in *de facto* uniforms of white shirts and black trousers, squirmy boys captive to their duties of copying and chanting ancient words. But their self-pity was itself a joke, because the two friends had also loved school, the diving deep into ancestral obscurities and resurfacing to show off their cleverness in passionate competition. Izzy's star had been rising faster, they both knew it, till he had been forced to leave when they were twelve.

Sixty years, give or take. Gershom had never seen or spoken to him again. He couldn't have when they were children, only able to go where their parents took them, find the people their families would let them find. It wasn't like today, when his little grandson from Sarah's first marriage could go on the Internet and discover how to make a pipe bomb. But, Rabbi Gershom confessed to himself in his empty office, he hadn't wanted to know Izzy for years after they parted. He'd been angry, righteously angry, and only later ashamed for wanting so much to be correct. And the shame had spread through the memory, like water finding the cracks in a badly built wall, so that eventually it seemed easier to let the whole thing crumble behind him and build anew.

A few times, over the decades, the rabbi had looked for his former friend's name in the news. He must have made something of himself. A writer, a historian, a teacher? His name was distinctive, but then, his father might have changed it, to give them a fresh start or aid his ascent in the civil service, where Russians were viewed as suspect. Abramoff's desultory research went nowhere.

THE HOUSE OF CORRECTION 85

He was daunted by the size of the world, the number of men in it committing crimes, writing books, lying dead for days in lonely apartments, fighting the Cold War, declaring their pride in doing unspeakable things with other men. Rabbi Gershom didn't want to know which of these fates was Izzy's.

Before he could lose his nerve, he wrote the name on a Post-It and took it out to Maya, the secretarial temp, who was filling in while his efficient Mrs. Lohmann was on medical leave. She was young, she could probably find anything on the Internet without breaking a nail. Things about himself he didn't even know. Talking to her felt strange, un-practiced. He'd been too alone all morning. He'd walk in the rain if necessary.

Maya turned the paper this way and that, squinting her wide hazel eyes like an archaeologist finding a fragment of hieroglyphics. Too vain to wear glasses, Rabbi Gershom groused internally. If she wasn't the board president's niece...

"Okay. What do you need this for?" she chirped.

Fresh, too. Taken aback, the rabbi said the first thing that came into his head. "For Sarah's wedding."

"Sure thing, I'll find his address and send him an invitation right away!"

Not a bad idea, come to think of it. A big party to buffer the awkwardness of their reunion. Gershom could watch him with others, sense his mood, maybe not even bring up the past this time around, not till they'd broken bread together and shared the warmth of wine. The sky was brightening, but he folded his umbrella under his arm as he left the building.

Weddings. Carla Zebatinsky, M.Sci., Ed.D., could take them or leave them. She could appreciate the Art Deco reception hall with its tulip-shaped chandeliers, the savory Swedish meatballs and Israeli wine brought to her by light-footed waiters, and the background jazz piano and strings. She could, honestly, relax into the not-Jewishness of it all, its untroubled richness. Her own reflection in the repeating mirrors was adequate: high-necked sleeveless russet cocktail dress, stiff satin pushing her curves into a younger shape, thick chestnut hair twisted up in a French braid instead of the utilitarian bun she wore to teach school. But when she was compelled to linger on the sight, fixing her sweat-smudged makeup in the ladies' room, she strained to see the Carla that Paige had seen. As if dumb glass, fused silica backed with silver, could tell her what glamour had temporarily covered her and then evaporated.

Carla was aware that Poppy pitied her. It was his way of pretending he lived in the nineteenth century. Daughters in his genre of ethnic tragedy reached an unfortunate age past which they were only fit to escort elderly relatives to parties. She and Natalie had decided long ago to keep the proofs to themselves of hot nights with friendly men who didn't have to stay. Then Beanie fell in love for real, and was gifted a few years of sweet calm before the aneurysm felled her on the laundry room floor, husband's unfolded boxers still in hand.

When the ushers at the ceremony had received them for sorting to bride's or groom's side, Poppy had eagerly

THE HOUSE OF CORRECTION   87

explained that Sarah Abramoff was his daughter's childhood friend. "Oh, were you at the Schechter school or
Camp Ramaz?" the bustling old lady asked Carla, and
Poppy corrected her that he meant his younger daughter,
Natalie, who couldn't be here today. Carla blinked twice
at this, his story already dropping an essential piece. But
she patted his gnarled hand, to show she was happy that
he was happy to be here, together looking on the bright
side of memories that could have hurt.

The couple of the moment said their brief vows under
the *chuppah* and cracked the traditional wineglass under-
foot. Carla didn't recognize them or anyone, and she had
plenty of practice memorizing faces each school year.
Her father cheered with the rest, his eyes watery. Then
the makeshift canopy was folded, the shards swept away,
and the celebration launched.

Contrary to Poppy's judgment of her, Carla could
have been picked to star in a scene like this several times
over. Last year, before Paige came to the school, she'd
broken off a two-year fling with an orthodontist she'd
met on JDate who was ready for her to have his babies.
Jason was a catch but it was the same thing all over again,
the wall she'd hit with the other men: they just didn't
feel *necessary*. She concluded she wasn't wired to feel the
surge that had flung Lara into Dr. Zhivago's arms, that
had bonded her mother to Poppy through the birth of
three children and death of one, then ruptured that bond
before Beanie's headstone was unveiled. (The former Mrs.
Zebatinsky was now married to a documentary producer
in Santa Barbara.) That had been Carla's hypothesis,
before Paige.

She was blonde. She was French — well, *Québéçoise* — and taught that subject down the hall from Carla's lab. Her mouth was strawberry-ice-cream pink, born the color of lipstick, without help, as Carla learned on that night they unlocked their cars in the dark, side by side in the school alley. The beginning and the ending didn't matter. In the middle was everything — oh, in the slippery center of her animal self, mirrored in the other, delving in tandem between shaking legs jumbled together in the janitor's closet. Words would undo this, but the woman traded in them. The masculine ending, the past tense verb. The promise to un-promise herself to the husband, who got a better job in Chicago and took Paige away at the end of term. The new year began in silence that Carla didn't expect to be broken.

Taking advantage of what she now knew to be her invisibility, her inconsequential being, Carla wove among the clusters of cocktail drinkers at the Abramoff-Shapiro wedding, on a mission to check up on Poppy. She hovered behind him as he chatted with a bright young couple at a banquet table, comparing their trips to Russia before and after the fall of the Iron Curtain. He was lively, engaged, holding their attention. Carla was about to join them when a cushiony grandmother got there first with her little girl in tow. Turning on the old-world charm, Poppy pulled out a chair for the woman, then entertained the toddler with his pocket watch and chain.

"Professor Zebatinsky taught with Dad at the Center for International Studies," Carla overheard the young man proclaim.

"Ah, no wonder you looked familiar," his mother greeted Poppy. "Were you still there when that woman Bamako became president?"

Poppy mimicked her disapproving eyebrow-raise. "She was quite a character."

Carla was confused, then worried, then angry. The old liar. How many different ways was he going to pretend to know these people? Yet someone had actually invited him, while she, the honest stranger, was nothing but a "plus one."

That, right there, was why she could not do anything as ridiculous as "come out" to him. Not that his dead Dostoevskyan God would care about the chromosomes of her bed partner. But that her discovery of herself had begun and ended in the same way this evening would end, with her extraneous to the pair-bonding of male and female, *l'dor va'dor*. Above the *chuppah*, an empty mirror on the wall.

In another corner of the noisy, gilded hall, Rabbi Gershom sank into an armchair with a glass of Scotch on the rocks. The rare moment to himself made room for sadness to surprise him. It wasn't about giving his daughter away. He'd done that before. Rabbi Gershom had come to terms with modern life and could agree that Sarah had always been her own property, not his. No, he was sad because two of his surviving classmates from Beit Tzedek were here: Ephraim the history professor, Dan the lawyer, their wives and some grown children.

Their lives were so full of things to talk about, it had been easy, second nature, not to mention Izzy or their teacher, Reb Solomon.

Solomon Bader had been their most popular instructor from the day he started at the yeshiva, when Gershom and Izzy were ten. Young and ruddy-cheeked in a school of grey-beards, with a proud nose and full black beard like the statues of Assyrian god-kings in their history books. He taught them to argue every side of a theory, till philosophy seemed like a spinning gem that could blind them with its winking facets. Reb Sol used his title in the classroom, but put the boys at ease after hours with the daring of a first-name friendship. More than half a century later, old Rabbi Gershom could recall the winey taste of the sticky dried fruit snacks Sol gave them, and the hot heaviness of his hand on Gershom's shoulder as he leaned over to correct a lesson.

But it was Izzy he favored at first, giving him extra tutoring for a public speaking competition that could win the yeshiva some money from a foundation. The boy's grades pulled ahead and he had less time to fool around with his friend. Geri, stung that he hadn't been tapped to compete, threw himself into his own work. Till then he'd foreseen his path as a scholar, like gentle Rabbi Avram, the oldest teacher, but the new Gershom set himself to becoming a smart speaker, humble volunteer, helper of slow learners — the school's brightest public face. And in some strange way the social tide turned against Izzy, who had become weary-eyed and nervous. When? His best friend hadn't noticed. All the boys were equally shocked when Izzy pulled out of the competition with an accusation that tore the school apart.

Even with a lifetime of pastoral counseling behind him, the grotesque idea made old Gershom shudder. His private strength, which he'd once been ashamed of, was that he could let his congregants' confessions rest on him like oil on the water's surface, to be skimmed off later, leaving everyone feeling clear and clean. Not so with the images of what Izzy whispered that Sol's hands, his *mouth*, had done — Rabbi Gershom, and the boy he had been, could feel it like fire ants on his skin.

And so he had not believed him. Did nothing to discourage their friends' rumors that Izzy was covering for some failure or family shame that would prevent him from representing the school. Or worse, that his false charge concealed desire for the teacher they idolized. A wish they could only speak of with the ancient word for abomination: *Toevah*.

Reb Sol moved on mid-year to another school in New Jersey. By then, Izzy had been gone for a month. One day he was just not there in his usual seat in front of Geri, winking over the back of the chair at the forgetful stutter of Rabbi Avram's chalk on the blackboard. His shy mother no longer joined them at the shul's monthly Shabbat dinner, baby daughter propped on her hip as she circled the table with a serving tray. Gershom flashed on a memory of the child's fat white hand knocking over a kiddish cup, the awkward pause before someone laughed out a blessing, the reddish-purple stain spreading across the paper tablecloth. And Izzy holding the girl on his lap, like a little old father.

They had believed they were men already. Wearing suits and fedoras, debating the laws of life and death in two languages. Rabbi Gershom's wife had never blessed him with sons, so this mental picture went unchallenged till Sarah had Matty, his first grandson. He was so small. Nine years old now. A child. Preoccupied with numbers, baseball scores, and battles in his computerized worlds. No normal man could look at his hairless freckled body and think of seduction. And if anyone dared suggest Matty were to blame for such a thing —

Toevah. Toevah.

Ronnie was bored with her family again. She'd said hello to everyone she knew at Cousin Sarah's wedding and helped herself to two plates of caviar. Now what? She liked the old gang, but they made her claustrophobic. She just hadn't expected the feeling to hit this early. Another hour or two and she could be riding her Harley along the beach road in the moonlight, the real reason she couldn't turn down an invite to Miami.

Families were good at seeing what they already knew, a limitation from which she wasn't exempt, to be fair. She put old thoughts in their heads and questions in their eyes when she strode past with her black tuxedo pants and jagged short hair, but maybe those thoughts had spun round so many times they'd worn themselves out and gone silent, like the Joan Jett record that kept her alive in middle school. Music, by contrast, was a practice of finding fresh truth in a replayed passage, even as Uncle Gershom claimed to do when he made the congregation listen to the same old fables about plagues and goats and favorite sons. Shaarei Tefilah called itself Conservative/Egalitarian, which meant things could be changed if they pretended it wasn't happening very fast. Men could dance with women because they were modern, and women with women because they were modest, and either way Ronnie had no excuse not to approach that smart-looking stranger with the rich brown hair and satin dress the color of a midnight kiss.

She waited impatiently till the vapid boy-pop of Justin Bieber gave way to Natasha Bedingfield's up-tempo "Pocketful of Sunshine." Ronnie couldn't lie about music, even to meet the only new prospect in town.

"This song always makes me want to dance. What about you?"

The woman in burgundy was surprised, but maybe, just maybe, dared to be pleased. "I don't know it, but I'll give it a try."

"I'm Sarah's cousin Ronit — Ronnie. How did you get mixed up with these people?"

Hesitation, then a belly laugh: "I have no idea." Thinking Ronnie was expecting more words, when it was really movement she longed for, her potential dance partner added, "I don't think we really belong here. My father got the invitation, but he won't admit he doesn't remember why."

"That's hilarious. Or is it sad?"

"You tell me!" The woman shrugged her shapely broad shoulders. Ronnie followed her glance in the direction of an old man with a thick neck and Beethoven hair, recounting a story to a young couple as they all refilled their vodka glasses. "At least he's enjoying himself."

"Well, now it's your turn," Ronnie said. And she grasped the woman's firm hand and pulled her forward, high heels clacking, onto the ballroom floor. They danced as if they knew the song, the steps, each other. Ronnie liked a woman who could sweat. Slower song, arm's length, talking now. One lived in Brooklyn, the other the Bronx. What were the odds? Ronnie was a sound engineer at music clubs. Carla taught angular momentum and gravitational attraction to teenagers. They could have a conversation longer than two sentences about the numbers underlying their lives not measured in babies, dress sizes, ages with and without foundation and blush.

But: the late hour, the ocean... "I've got a crazy idea," she told Carla, as if it were new. She would lend Carla her jacket. They'd stash her tottering shoes in the compartment where she kept the spare helmet. No matter how many times in the history of motorcycles this had happened before, the moonlight would be clear as ever, and the waves refreshing on the sand between their toes, each one changing the coastline just a little bit, adding and taking away.

Carla probably didn't think of herself as impulsive, Ronnie guessed, but here she was, crashing the wedding of a rabbi's daughter. Second wedding, but that was still two more than the good people of Florida would allow Ronnie's kind to have. A stray chestnut tendril, sprung loose from her French braid, stuck to Carla's forehead. Ronnie could only brush it aside in her imagination.

"But Poppy — someone should look after him —" Her voice was wistful. She was ready to delegate. She just needed Ronnie's help.

"Here, I know." Ronnie scanned the ballroom: who was still solo, not yet drunk or in love? "Uncle Gershom looks like he needs a drinking buddy. They're about the same age, seventies, right? Let's introduce them. Unless your father has already told him he's Elie Wiesel's cardiologist or something."

Carla chuckled; guilty, but hooked. The night opened up, a smooth silver road. They would let the rabbi know where the Zebatinskys' hotel was, and would he please help Isaac into a taxi if he got tired before his daughter returned from her walk? Ask him to do what he loved best, caretake the confused. The dimmed lights winked at their doubles in the dark window glass, little golden moons beckoning them to cross over to the outdoors.

Halfway through an anecdote about Beanie and Jeremy's tenth-anniversary vacation in Tel Aviv, Zebatinsky forgot it wasn't true. Noticed, stopped and resumed, encouraged by the clarifying warmth of his drink, like the glassy sunshine of those desert days. The scent of ripening pomegranates was real, and the sky's unforgiving swimming-pool blue, and the mad drivers on twisted old streets. Except he'd been there alone, at an academic conference on some vanished topic, in the first year of his loss. And why hadn't it been Natalie in his story that was actually also true (except for its protagonist), if not for an eye-blink of that idiot God who had sent a wandering goat into the road to shield the tourist woman from a reckless motorbike?

Zebatinsky had seen the traffic-stopping drama through his rental car's dusty windshield: the young woman shocked and grateful, furious and laughing, all in a moment, before she released herself into her husband's arms and let him feel strong again. That was so like Beanie, the way she gave you the gift of needing you, though you both knew she could survive on the air and nectar of life itself. The baby in the husband's backpack carrier could have been the one she and Jeremy planned, not the unblossomed blob of tissue her womb had housed when her brain spasmed.

Why, then, on this tropical evening, in this crowd of well-wishers, why shouldn't they have that future that their family had almost touched? Zebatinsky would never see these good people again. Unlikely, moreover, that they'd recall his tale sufficiently to fact-check it later, should their paths recross. Feelings were the essence.

He understood why not, of course. Like falling asleep in the false warmth of snow on the steppe, that way led to exile, imprisonment, the benevolent propaganda machine of senility. His ancestors kept their humanity by clinging to the hardest truths. But for once he was tempted to let history slide off his shoulders, stop resisting the hushed and carpeted resting place that Carla urged him toward.

Suddenly a short, stout old man with a trim straw-colored beard rushed up to him, clasping his arm, jostling his drink. Zebatinsky blinked several times before he recognized the rabbi, the father of the bride, the very man he'd seen under the *chuppah* a couple of hours ago. This slow recall didn't worry him as much as it would have before the vodka. The other man, however, was quite agitated, his eyes moist behind gold-rimmed spectacles.

"Izzy? Do you remember me — Geri, from Beit Tzedek?"

No one had called him Izzy since — well, since before his bar mitzvah, surely. The rabbi's incompletely suppressed accent called up echoes of a New York childhood. Zebatinsky could picture the name on the wedding invitation now. "Gershom... Geri," he pronounced slowly, and smiled. He *did* belong here.

Taking this for recognition, Gershom burst into shocking tears. Both hands seized his. "Izzy, I believe you! I *do*. I should have spoken up, all those years ago. Can you forgive me?"

A chill of fear sobered up the old professor. His audience had dispersed, granting them privacy for this strange reunion. "F-forgive?" he stammered.

"I loved our teacher, you understand? We all did. I couldn't face that he would — do that, that bad thing to you. But I was your friend. I should have known better."

This was terrible. Zebatinsky's gut burned. He understood exactly what the rabbi was too squeamish to name. These days it was all over the news, a guaranteed topic for campus literary magazines and freshman composition essays. Zebatinsky himself had had a hinky feeling about his son's tennis coach and transferred the boy to a different summer camp, using cost as an excuse. But this evil had never touched him personally — *had it?* Crazy, crazy thought. One heard of such induced oblivion only in ridiculous American spy movies, a young healthy mind (not his gently, deliberately fogged one) lightning-wiped by a secret shock. If — solely for purposes of argument — if Zebatinsky's life story, unbeknownst to him, resembled the *National Enquirer* more than *The Death of Ivan Ilyich*, he would continue to be happier not knowing. Easiest thing in the world to tell poor Gershom that all was forgiven, and go find sulky Carla to call them a taxi.

But looking anew into the rabbi's stricken, expectant face, Zebatinsky felt the contrariness of his ancestors rise in him, their stubborn preservation of unpopular prophesies. Letting out a long breath, he said, in a voice that for the first time sounded reed-thin to his own ears, "Geri... I have had a long life. A good life, though my heart has been broken. I've forgotten many things that I used to think were so important. It's too late for me to tell you whether what you did was wrong or right. I didn't even know why you sent me this invitation. To me, it's as if we met for the first time tonight."

Thus unburdened, having admitted the weakness he most feared, Zebatinsky was suffused with peace, mixed with pride at his wisdom. He gripped that fluttering bird of enlightenment rather tightly in his mind, as it threatened to escape the annoying embrace of Rabbi Gershom, dampening his shirt front with relieved sobs.

Speed, and space, and bare skin in the wind. Carla careened toward the ocean under the enormous sky, nothing binding her to safety except her arms around this woman, this Ronnie, at the front of the roaring bike. Out here in the open, away from buildings and crowds, the cosmic whirl and lines of force she studied were more than a theory. And when they finally stopped, as she'd anticipated they would, to strip off their shoes and stockings and walk unsteadily along the ocean-licked edge of the sand, it almost made her giggle to imagine the moon's tidal power drew the water just for her, like a father pulling a warm blanket over his child's feet.

Whatever else happened, moments like this were to be seized. Her family's history had taught her that. Ronnie might pull a "Freebird" and ride out of her life, tomorrow or months from now when Carla started day-dreaming about two-bedroom apartments and artificial insemination, but she, Carla, would henceforth always be someone chosen, someone who had said yes to herself.

Walking slowed to sitting on a bank of sea grass under some stubby canted trees, squeezed hip to hip on Carla's spread-out pashmina shawl to keep the salt stains from their formal clothes. Paige's kisses had been furtive, enticing, with the repeated pretense of a surprising, irresistible fall. Ronnie's were direct and eager as a boy's, but sisterly soft, her breaths matching Carla's ebb and flow.

Some teenagers had lit a driftwood fire along the shore. The women listened to it sputter and crackle, leaning on each other, not needing to push their closeness further yet. "How did you know...I'd do this?" Carla murmured.

"First thing when we get back to New York, I'm buying you a gaydar detector." Ronnie chuckled. "No, seriously... you never *know* anyone. Not across the proverbial crowded room, not on your thirtieth anniversary. But I'm a gambler. And you — a single woman, at this gold-plated heterosexual love-fest, who's not lining up to dance with every divorced groomsman and doctor's brother — you didn't need to force your way into their circle. That got my interest."

"I wish... I don't think I'm that independent person you saw. That's Poppy, who could be perfectly happy with nothing but a bookshelf full of dead Russians. In a couple years he may be talking to the pigeons but he'll believe they're hanging on his every word about narrative structure in *The Cherry Orchard*."

"And you want to grab the mike for a change?"

"Not even. I guess I just want to be myself, and for it to matter that it's *me* listening."

"It's very clear to me," Ronnie said, tracing her finger along the curve of Carla's breast, "that you're not a pigeon."

Did you mean...

On that gusty January day a month before, Maya had been perplexed by the search results on her screen. The temp had translated the cramped writing on Rabbi Gershom's Post-It note into nice clear keystrokes, but the person they conjured up did not sound like the ideal wedding guest.

Showing results for 'izaac zebatinsky'

...Izaac Zebatinsky, two-time winner of the American Psychological Association's Farber Book Award for <u>Befriending Yourself</u> *and* <u>Hearing What Your Child Can't Say</u>*...*

...raised over $50,000 to bring the families to the U.S., said Izaac Zebatinsky, chairman of the synagogue's Soviet Jewry relief committee...

<u>School Counselor Sentenced in Abuse Case</u> *[Staten Island Advance] Nov. 17, 1998... Izaac Zebatinsky, 57, a family therapist in private practice and former counselor at the Grinspoon Day School...*

<u>People vs. Zebatinsky</u> *...Decided on March 8, 2007 County Court, Richmond County (NY)... A hearing was held to determine the level of risk the defendant Izaac Zebatinsky presents to re-offend... convicted in 1998 of two counts of Sexual Abuse in the First Degree, Person Incapable of Consent by Reason of Age (less than eleven years old)... The court recommends that Level 2 Offender Status continue...*

Maya peered at the yellow slip of paper again, then back to the monitor, where the search engine was helpfully offering her an out:

<u>*Also show results for 'isaac zebatinsky'*</u>

Perhaps she'd read it wrong. "Isaac" *was* the normal spelling. The letter was so small, a minimal curl of ink connecting the swooping "I" and the slanted-closed bumps of the "a's." Since no one was around to see her, she popped open the drawer where she stashed her reading glasses, those outdated round frames that made her look (she thought) like a goggle-eyed mosquito. The doctor had promised her contacts would be ready next week, then no more of these headaches.

Maya opened a new window and clicked back and forth, back and forth between the two photos she'd found. The author, the professor. The criminal, the one who... well, you never knew, right? And what was with these old Russian guys and their Einstein hairdos? Not like Rabbi Gershom, who was hot stuff for a grandpa, though kind of short. She wanted to show him she could do this job. No more asking dumb questions.

Once she'd copied the address onto the invitation, she cleared her search history (her boss didn't need to know what she was looking up on WebMD), turned out the lights, and went home.

MEMORIES OF THE SNOW QUEEN

THE STORY OF THE SNOW QUEEN BEGINS WITH A DEMON. An imp, we're corrected, because this is a story for, or at least about, children. Imps are for impulse, as A is for apple, as I is for ice. They're too young to try out the demon's repertoire of fiery touches, black silk stockings, suicide songs. The imp's craving is merely for mischief. He's a little boy who says *No*.

A demon, or an imp if you will, is a good reason to start a story. Something demands explanation, cause is sought and blame is found. The mirror on the wall, intact as an unwed princess, need not be discussed. The mirror on the floor, shattered into grit that sticks in the eye, arrowheads lodged in the arch of the foot, a splinter in the palm — this, now, demands someone else tell of a *who* and a *why* that the smashed reflector cannot disclose.

So the imp threw the looking glass out of heaven, we're told, and a grain of the sand of its disintegration worked its way into the yard of a cottage where a boy and a girl were playing at being in love like two daffodils on the same stalk. Perhaps the unseen scratch made a bead of blood spring up on his fingertip, and without understanding he felt their play spoiled and another old story begun in its place — the one about disobedience, sleep, and thorns. Perhaps he rubbed his eye with a dirty boy-fist and the garden looked darker, the leaves' desiccated future in embryo in their green, the chocolate soil seeded with mouse bones. And he became angry at the girl's cow eyes and her prattle like raindrops in a churchyard, even more when she wept at the new scowl on her dear playmate's face, as if a boy could do anything but bare his puppy teeth at a world where broken glass fell from the sky.

But when the shard reached his heart, all this changed again. He breathed it in, we're corrected, there was no wound. Around the bit of mirror, the bit his body hadn't made but was fast disappearing into his tissues, the white blood cells rushed in, clumping like snowflakes, turning to ice. Plates of ice like a white knight's armor, floors and rooms of ice spreading a ballroom over black water, so thick even the worst little boy could stamp his feet hard and not plunge through to the pants-wetting chill. He was a giant who could cast winter on the world.

It was then that the Snow Queen first arrived at the edge of the pine forest where the yard ended.

Or: It was then that the boy was first able to see the Snow Queen distinct from the crystal-swagged boughs and pillowed drifts encircling the children's shared play, her cold finer than their cold, the gleaming facets of her jeweled fingers more alluring than the sharpest icicle he'd ever stuck to his foolish tongue.

Or: It was then that the boy first stopped being able to see the Snow Queen, like a front door he had faced all his life that was now behind him.

Whatever way this turn of the story is told, with the next breath the boy was swept up into the carriage of the Snow Queen and disappeared from the girl's sight as completely as a gaggle of popular girls closing around their new pet. Some versions say the boy himself chose to take that ermine seat, but how could he have lifted his body up to that porcelain chassis steep as a claw-foot tub, with the ice stiffening his veins? Some versions say he'd always belonged to the Snow Queen, but these leave out the mirror and the imp, and are less reliable.

Color floods the story like mulled cider as the boy evaporates into the blue realms of motive and the girl pours herself into her quest. There are the steaming turf-brown pelts of reindeer and the cindery laughter of crows, and the broad-shouldered robber girl with eyes like crackling coals, who comforts her in a bed canopied by the linty fluttering of pigeons, and stashes a knife under the pillow. But let's backtrack a moment. Does no one at home care to keep this girl in sight, in the yard from which another child has presumably been stolen? Why is she free to journey toward the fortress of winter, paying back the guiding river with her red shoes?

We're told her innocence is what makes the northern landscape bend to help her, such that the very roses return from underground to reassure her about the dead. But how she could have grown to walking age with such a heart, in a house with no more than a sleeping grandmother, that placeholder of old tales, to teach her about love? Well, this may seem improbable even in a story where many things remain unexplained.

If we give the girl the real sort of family that produces trusting children, with predictable mealtimes and parents paired like the lame crow and his sweetheart, we might believe the version that says she never strayed far from the yard, that there was no mystery and no need for a journey, only a snow-softened memory of an afternoon when her playmate fell ill and his mother came out to carry him upstairs in her white fur coat that smelled like a grown-up party: tobacco and perfume and hair. The girl's parents, or the boy's mother, wouldn't let her visit him for some time, in case he was contagious. Does it make sense that they never again played so closely together, after that day? That's how she remembers it.

In this version, which doesn't seem like a story at all, the girl winds her way through the usual course of prom-night gropes and cold hands meeting around a coffee-shop paper cup, to a shared mattress in a loft where smoke and misquoted philosophers thicken the dawn air, stars fading through the open casement like lopsided snowflakes melting on a sleeve. She lives close to her parents, who are good people and generous about inviting her friends to dinner, not asking too many questions. When did the boy and his mother move away? She used to think about him more often, when she had a babysitting job that took her past the yard where they'd played, though oddly she has no memory of him living in that bluish-white house where his mother had arrived so quickly on the scene to put him to bed. The mother, too, she can picture only in splintered pieces: a pouf of frosted blonde, a ring forced over a knuckle, its square, diamond-like stone.

The girl takes classes to become a veterinary technician. The frogs arrive in bags at each lab bench. The biology freshmen slide out their knives from their cushioned cases, preparing to sort the diagrammed organs into piles, to confirm what's already known. Poised over the splayed amphibian, its flung-back head and soft belly pinked by formaldehyde, the girl is suddenly certain she ran upstairs into the house, behind the boy and his mother, the day he fell ill in the yard. Though she hadn't been invited, she was sure, in fact she didn't think she'd ever been allowed inside before, odd as that sounds, or else why would she have become so lost among corridors lined with spine-cracked books and rooms with overstuffed couches that seemed too white, too huge, too still, like slumbering polar bears?

Surely it was only minutes before she reached the bathroom, if indeed she had been there at all, and saw the boy's hand flopped over the edge of the tub, his mother still in her fur coat for some reason, sponging him with cold water. *To bring down his fever*, the woman said, drawing an ice cube over his forehead, down between his closed eyes, his purpled lips, his throat, as the girl is watching her lab partner unzip her frog like a change purse. As the boy lay in the greening water that rippled and blurred his skin, as the mother reached into the bag of ice that seemed to be in an inner pocket of her fur coat, to plaster a soothing handful over the sick child's heaving breastbone, the girl's gaze followed the motion of that ringed hand to his small penis nested between his pale legs, so curious, his secret strange and familiar, wrong and right. The mother, with eyes that might have been sled-dog blue or December black with the knowledge of everything, saw the girl and the girl knew she knew, was found out in her filth, and now there was no one to ask if any of this had been true, because of course she hadn't told her parents, who were good people and would not like her imagining such things at her age.

In the story that the children had acted out together, playing in that long-ago yard, the Snow Queen was not at home when the journeying girl, the shoeless girl, the motherless girl walked into the icicle palace to wash the broken mirror out of the boy's heart with her tears, which were hot as broth fed to a bedridden child. The boy, we're told, didn't see her right away, or he saw her and it meant nothing, which comes to the same thing, as one puzzle piece is indifferently like its fellow until one finds the right edge where no other will fit.

He was laboring over alphabet blocks of ice, repeating his failure to spell the word the Snow Queen had promised they made, which was *Eternity*, for if he succeeded he should sit on her ermine throne forever and have a new bicycle, though in truth it would only be new for a small part of that long reign. Possibly the Snow Queen was even dead, because she was certainly older than the boy, and he thought sometimes he had been at the blocks for years. But it seemed unlikely, in this blue north where fruit neither smelled nor softened, that anyone could die who had been alive to begin with. Without the ice around the glass from the imp in his heart, the boy could have been angry that the Snow Queen had not cared to stay and see him complete the task she had begun.

Perhaps, then, the girl's first act was not to weep. For who can do another's weeping for him? She could, instead, have picked up some of that frozen alphabet, till their four hands, skinned and scarred with cold, had spelled out this story, or another even more clear.

TAKING DOWN
THE PEAR TREE

You agree to her naming the baby maurice. it's after a character in a novel you've never read, a book that (Wikipedia tells you) has a tragic but miraculous ending. You found such stories embarrassing in high school, twenty years ago, probably the last time you tried to read a novel by someone dead. The guilty rash on the minister's chest, the Christmas ghosts. Your imitations got the B-minuses they deserved. But you can't bite your lips through another winter of songs about angels bringing babies to pure girls. Your arms ache. This is a real thing. You try to work your mouth around the name — soft, loud, in your childhood's Brooklyn accent, in your Connecticut suburb's lack of one — till it sounds like something a boy would be willing to answer to when you called him home.

Your husband goes through nicknames to reassure himself. Not Maury, an old uncle who tells bad jokes. Not Moe, cartoon bartender, stooge. But Reese is a fine name for a first-round draft pick or patent attorney. He could co-sign a mortgage, tie his own shoes.

Your husband's name is Thomas. Everyone calls him Thomas.

It is January. The specialist's rubber finger widens your crack, probes the hollow she sees between stirrups. She has short pale hair and rimless glasses and a Polish name that your husband jokes sounds like "paycheck." He is not in the room. The numbers on her screen look good to her. On the walls are the usual red cross-sections of female muscle and Impressionist sailboats. The paper sheet crackles like a fire under you, heat sweeping over your skin, crushing you breathless. She doesn't understand why you're not pregnant. Your heart rate is high. *Does anything hurt?* You feel the walls of your womb contracting, shrinking from the speculum, gathering the wishful strength to expel it so they can join forever like scar tissue, a marriage that excludes a third. *Nothing hurts*, you say.

After you're dressed, the specialist brings Thomas back and shows the two of you her hopeful charts. Your age plus number of embryos implanted equals probability. And what of the others? You use the A-word to show how tough-minded you are. No euphemistic *reductions* for you. Thomas half-closes his eyes wisely, the face that looks like listening but only you know means patient disagreement. Eye contact would throw off his game, so you devote your attention to his lion-fur eyebrows, the wide furrows of his forehead, which you truly cherish, though there are limits on what you will do to make a next-generation copy. The fresh panties you brought for after the procedure feel damp and used. You're afraid you smell. Thomas stands so you stand. He shakes her hand

and tucks the handout under his arm. Your husband was raised Catholic. You hope he remembers that.

You drive too fast to the Cracker Barrel. Both of you order chicken pot pie and syrupy iced tea. Thomas sits with his back to the fireplace because you're still sweaty, despite the whip of snow in the air outdoors. He says this might be the year he runs for City Council. Someone has to take a strong stand on stormwater management. He's a financial planner, but the market is slow. You relax into the familiar topics. The year stretches ahead like the interstate, straight and bare under white winter sun.

All the next week you dream thick, dark dreams, itching under a knit blanket you almost recognize — an aunt's house, a friend's? Washing breakfast dishes, you say aloud the name of a discontinued lipstick: *Berry Chic*, a Kool-Aid color in a mashed tube you shared with your ninth-grade best friend Mira, swapping tastes of wax and spit. You say her name, relieved to be certain of something. You're glad the house is empty.

There is a room that is blue and green.
There is a room whose door is always closed.

You and your friend Pauline and the new guy, Glenn, run an executive staffing firm downtown. You match résumés to positions at insurance agencies, law offices, nursing homes, and the occasional quirky client like the holistic spa or the boarding school for deaf kids. It's the same pleasure as filling in a crossword puzzle. Pauline's mother never worked and yours, of course, had to stop early. You're satisfied by the sight of yourself in the washroom mirror, pearl studs or gold knots in your ears, champagne-beige dress or black pants suit, some blouse that doesn't show sweat. Though it's been awhile since you talked about it, you know Pauline, adjusting her headband beside you, feels the same.

It is March. The social worker asks why you want to have a baby. Thomas is sitting in the chair next to yours, but she is only looking at you. You think, not for the first time, that no one asks men this question. The mere willingness to become a father on purpose, and to expend some effort to do so, automatically puts Thomas on the good-conduct list. He is responsible, respectable, unselfish. Unfortunately, this is all true, so you can't take out your frustrations on him. Besides, from now on, you'll have to present a united front.

You could tell her that Thomas talked you into reactivating your adoption application when he caught you crying in front of the Easter egg dye kits at the supermarket. *The problem with our life,* he'd said, *is that we have no liturgical calendar.* You don't talk this way, and you can't take the chance that this new social worker will think you're being pretentious or flippant. But you'd instantly understood what he meant: the feeling that none of it applies to you, as your neighbors and the

114   *JENDI REITER*

people on TV cycle through back-to-school sales, letters to Santa, Mother's Day bouquets.

You could tell her you want someone to love. You could tell her you want immortality. Someone who needs you. Not only do these sound like the terrible song lyrics you and Mira wrote when you were both crushing on that sophomore with the electric guitar, they are unbelievably self-centered, as is anything you might say about someone who doesn't exist yet.

You tell her the truth you have both rehearsed: that your marriage produces a creative energy that you want to share. That it's not in the cards for you to create with your bodies, but a family is really made by love. The social worker gives you a binder of printouts from other couples' websites. She instructs you to start collecting photos of your life. Pictures for a story that a birthmother would want her child to be part of, other than her own.

Any moment, the call could come.
Rush to the hospital half-dressed, food uneaten.
The room must be made ready. The clothes laid out.
Cooling shades of green and blue.

Late night in the screen's glow, your neat kitchen in shadow. Click. Last summer's beach trip with your brother scrolls past. You find the one where you're building a sandcastle with his girlfriend's children. Click. Boston Christmas, at the theater with Thomas's parents. Your mother-in-law squints and sparkles in the camera's flash, crimson beaded sweater set not quite a match for her creased smiling lips. Click. Here's a good one, only a couple years old, you and Thomas under the white flowering tree on your front lawn. One can see how nice the house is from here, large enough but with cozy angles. Frowning a little, you wish you'd researched more-repellent bulbs after the deer beheaded your tulips. You know the colors of plants but not much else. Keeping track of your cervical mucus was all the Mother Nature business you had time for. Her other creatures' reproductive cycles would have to take care of themselves.

Click. They want your history. You pause over the icon for a half-minute, then open the folder where Thomas scanned the photos of your pre-digital childhood. Click, double-click. You haven't needed to look at these in so long. They've waited for you like the uncensored *Perrault's Fairy Tales* that you'd made your mother hide in her room, even the closed book giving you goosebumps, till you outgrew both the fear and the need to shock yourself afresh with a peek at its woodcuts of hungry giants and wolves.

Your mother stretches painlessly in the sunlight, steadying your little brother at the top of the slide. You're ignoring them, concentrated on walking your fat-legged plastic doll along the monkey bars. Probably your aunt took this one. The low-resolution, reddened Polaroid fuzzes your mother's summer-blonde curls, blurs her eyes behind outdated round pink eyeglasses that throw back the light. Now you're older than she was then. You always will be.

It is May. You have fielded a small number of strange phone calls. No wonder, when the vacant position in your family is now on the Internet with a toll-free line. Adoption is nothing like *Penny Serenade*, where the starched nurse handed Irene Dunne and Cary Grant a neat white bundle left on a doorstep by the stork. Thomas's depressed cousin Bridget came into his family that way, taken by nuns from a nameless unwed girl. He wants the opposite, no secrets. Two families joined by the gift of a child. He buys a picture book about it.

You don't let him see how you grit your teeth while taking notes on yet another call that will go nowhere, hating these girls' slow, confused voices, their rambling stories about everything but the baby, their phones that never pick up when you call back. Pauline commiserates with you about the general brain-deadness of young adults, as evidenced by her latest batch of interviewees, which is close enough on-topic to feel sympathetic.

It stuns you how much you want this all of a sudden. Waiting in line at the bank, you stare at the back of the woman ahead of you, who has a red-faced infant in a strap-on carrier peering grumpily over her shoulder. Your body can feel his heat and boneless weight, as though he nestled against your own chest. Forget your briefcase and high heels. You're a cave woman eyeing the last piece of raw mammoth.

You're in the hardware store looking at weed killers when your cell phone rings. Hurriedly you dig in your purse for a pen, then yank a handful of hazmat information sheets from the plastic pocket on the shelf, to take notes on their blank backs.

This girl, Lana, is different. Her voice is low and throaty, educated, serious but in control of her sadness, you think. She's four-and-a-half months pregnant. Right now she's waiting tables and teaching ESL part-time in Springfield, where some of her family lives. Her on-again, off-again boyfriend is an installation artist. You pretend to know what that means.

You mention the Basketball Hall of Fame, the only positive thing you remember about Springfield, one of the struggling post-industrial cities of Western Massachusetts. Lana doesn't follow basketball. She's just been accepted into a creative writing graduate program in New York City. It's not a good time to have a baby. She just couldn't go through another abortion. You honestly say you understand, without reciprocating details. She might agree that you don't deserve a child this time. But everyone has them, right? Something like forty-one percent of women. The moment to share this has passed. You take down Lana's number to call back when you get home, so you and Thomas can schedule a weekend to drive up to meet her and Blaine, the boyfriend.

As you try to stand up from the hard coil of garden hose you've been squatting on, your knees shake. The rubber fumes trapped in the narrow aisle make you stagger, like an anesthesia hangover.

———

Time is not on your side. Enough of your current and former friends have had babies that you know what happens to a mother's house. There'll never be a moment afterward, not for years, for you to clean the refrigerator. Every expired bottle of hot sauce and dusty opened tin of cocoa mix crashes into the kitchen bin. You scrub tacky red stains — strawberries? meat? — from the shelves, so vigorously they squeak in protest.

You can't stop there. Why do you have so many magazines? What is Thomas going to do with ten-year-old issues of *The Economist?* Libraries won't take them anymore. You stack them in a box at the curb, hoping they'll be free-cycled before rain turns them into a sad pulp. Your shoe closet annoys you, the scuffed and lopsided evidence of walking round and round the circuit of your days. Two trips to the thrift shop make you feel lighter. Thomas suggests a support group. Doesn't he understand how much space children take up? The bottle warmers, the bouncy seats, the two-foot-tall teddy bears that distant relatives will send to show the extravagance of their love? He agrees the house could use a spring cleaning. He brings his old sneakers to the dump.

The hospital brochure with the logo of the birthing center lies on your placemat on the kitchen table when you come home from work the next day. There are groups for infertility, bereavement, and parents waiting for an adoption or foster care placement. You will never again sit in a circle in a numbered small room where thick carpeting and piped-in Vivaldi ensure that the sounds of sorrow are muffled to the outside world. A real support group should be held in a cemetery, or a junkyard, where you could smear dirt on your body, rip your clothing, and smash windshields with a crowbar. You will never again express this opinion to a professional comforter who will look at you kindly, saying nothing. You get back in your car and drive to the post office because you can't think of anyplace more private to recycle the brochure. That's what it's come to.

It is still May. Thomas is anxious about parking the car in Springfield. He circles past the Spanish-language newsstand and the bus depot on its concrete island between vacant lots. *Relax,* you tell him. You find a spot in front of a well-kept red brick church from the last century, next door to a boarded-up department store. It reminds you of where you lived in Brooklyn after your dad left, only with fewer people on the streets in the daytime.

You already think highly of Lana for choosing this neighborhood coffee bar, one of the few holdouts against DD and Starbucks. A flyer taped to the window advertises last weekend's spoken-word performance night. You scan the warm brown-tinted room. No one looks eager to see you. A skinny young man in a black long-sleeved sweater and cut-off jeans slouches behind a laptop. The woman beside him happens to turn in your direction, then says something to her companion and rises, taking her time. Her straight black hair swings with the graceful movement of her small head on her elongated neck. She wears a faded green cotton print dress over black leggings, her strawberry mouth the only bold color.

Are you — ? She says your names. Her handshake is firm and cool. Thomas, eager for the occupation, takes drink orders. You blink your eyes downward, discreetly you hope, to the soft curve rounding out the fabric below her flat chest. He's in there. She's told you it's a boy. Your skin prickles with electricity, like the first time you saw a rock concert, or a dead body.

Closer up, they're older than you supposed from the phone calls. Blaine sprawls in his chair with teenage languor, but his blue eyes have squint lines and his reddish-blond curls might be thinning in back. The yeasty smell of his seasonally mismatched clothes is too intimate; it disturbs you. Lana can't be more than five years younger than you. *Six*, she says, with a little white smile that shows space between her front teeth. So, still skirting the edge of her twenties, a time to believe there'll be other choices, other children, waiting for her in the next decade.

Thomas and Blaine are quickly absorbed in comparing cell phones. They tinker with the settings on Blaine's laptop so he can show video clips of his art, which seem to consist of people moaning in oddly lit rooms. You and Lana bond by rolling your eyes at them. At least it's not sports talk.

She scoots her chair nearer you, shoulder to shoulder. Her breath is bitter cinnamon from the foamy cup she cradles in both hands. *You're so lucky*, she says, *to have grown up in the city.* Meaning New York, of course, there is no other. *The bookstores everywhere, the museums. And the Brooklyn Bridge —* She quotes what sounds like a poem, about ferries and flood-tides. *Did you ever feel like Whitman*, she asks, *did you ever look at all the people coming and going over the river, and imagine you were dead but part of something that went on and on?*

Sharp as tears, the sight comes back to you, of steel-gray water meeting white sky, where you'd let your mind drift like a child's lost balloon as the family car crawled to school or the doctor's office. You say yes, you wish you'd had a word for it. She looks at you. *It isn't just one thing. That's the point.*

For a moment you think she's going to lay her hand over yours, but she's smoothing down the smock over her belly, the first acknowledgment of why you're all here. *I've been thinking about names,* she says. *If it'd been a girl, I'd have wanted Sarah, but I'm glad it's a boy. So, Maurice.*

The men are looking at her now. *They're from 'The End of the Affair,'* she tells Thomas — because she thinks you already know? or will agree to anything? If this is a dig at Blaine, he takes it in stride. Back to you: *What books are you reading?* There's a little lisp in her voice, maybe from the parted teeth.

Your mind goes blank, then refills with nonsense. Last month when you had the flu, you lay in bed and sniffled your way through a Jodi Picoult novel about teen suicide. On your desk at work, you've got that book about the seven highly effective habits, but you can't remember what they are. Lying. Lying is definitely one of them.

David Copperfield, you tell Lana. You've seen two different PBS adaptations and you had the Classic Comics version as a child. Plus, it's lengthy enough that you won't be pressed for more titles on your reading list before the baby is born.

Thomas acts as if this is a normal conversation. No double-takes, no conspirators' glances. He doesn't expect to know everything about you. He's the kind of father you want Maurice to have.

————————————

When your mother was dying, you'd hide at Mira's house in the dark winter afternoons, pretending to do your English homework in her bed that didn't smell like rubbing alcohol or unwashed hair, where the only spills were sticky-sweet sloshes of Pepsi she'd doctored with a capful of rum from her dad's top shelf. Your teacher was pushing you both to apply for a junior year summer abroad program: Mira who actually deserved it, with her stories in the school magazine, and you, you suspected, out of pity. It would be all over by then. Everyone knew it over here, but in Cambridge you could just be a girl who handed in her papers on time and looked the right way, which was the wrong way, when crossing the street. So you really tried for a little while to keep the Catherines straight in *Wuthering Heights* and act shocked by the breakdown of society in *Lord of the Flies*, as if you and Mira didn't know too well the wild pig nature of boys.

Though you were both too old for make-believe, time and again you'd wind up together under Mira's blanket, balancing a flashlight and a shot glass, reading aloud the best, saddest bits of *Jane Eyre*. She was Helen at the cruel boarding school and would say the lines about loving her enemies and longing for heaven, and you were young

Jane arguing that God would want children to fight for their lives, or at any rate you were going to.

Then you would kiss each other sweetly, just like in the book, and make as though to fall asleep embracing. Mira said girls kissed on the lips all the time in Victorian literature. It was okay because you were young and innocent. You supposed Helen and Jane were too poor to have the corsets and petticoats that would have kept their small breasts and hungry bellies from rubbing together under the hot blanket, as yours and Mira's did. She usually did fall asleep because she was a lightweight, one spiked soda and that was it. In the real story, Helen is dead when Jane wakes up, cold with a smile on her face that Jesus put there. Mira was always warm, a bit grouchy after dozing, needing to pee and take an aspirin. Each time you told yourself it would be the last but it wasn't, yet.

Neither of you got the Cambridge scholarship. Mira was hired as a summer camp counselor in the Poconos where she met a boy and lost her virginity for real this time. She said the stuff she'd done before didn't count. Your dad let you stay with him in Miami for a couple of weeks, but there was nothing much to do because he slept most of the day and played music in clubs at night. You came home to your aunt, bought some suits, took data-entry classes.

It is not upon you alone the dark patches fall,
The dark threw its patches down upon me also —

It is July. Thomas has green paint in his hair. He doesn't own a baseball cap, and the stocking cap he was wearing to renovate the nursery got too hot. He's done the walls in a pale shade the hardware store called sage, the ceiling and baseboard white, with slate-blue blinds to dim the sun at naptime. Simple and subdued, that's what you both like. He wonders if there should be more ducks. You say it's fine. Lana is supposed to visit next month. She won't go in for clichés.

You indulge in other ways. You sniff the bunny feet of new fleecy pajamas, anticipating that baby smell added to the freshness of washed cotton. You discover books meant to be read with one's fingers, stroking the fine ridges of cardboard train tracks and the tufts of fake puppy fur. At last there's almost nothing to stop you from falling into the ocean of sentiment that you've skirted for so long. The whole world celebrates your right to drift, to sink.

At work you're closing out projects for existing clients and handing off new ones to Glenn and Pauline. Some afternoons you don't have much to do. David Copperfield has bitten his mean stepfather's hand and been shipped off to the boys' version of Jane Eyre's boarding-school prison. He doesn't know yet whether he will be the hero of his own life. Glenn spies the thick paperback on your desk, bookmarked near the beginning, and jokes that you'll never finish it by September. *Say bye-bye to reading once the baby comes.* You make yourself smile, because you still own half the firm. You can fire him someday if Pauline agrees. He must have no idea of the hungry hours that open up when you're caring for someone round the clock, to fill with turned pages and muted lip-read movies because you can't sleep, alert for the next cry.

When you dare to imagine yourself with baby Maurice, the scene is the dead of night, both of you sobbing with relief from the adults' daylight duty of cheerful functioning. Maurice won't know that people are not supposed to eat at four a.m., scream when they're confused, throw up on their clothes. You could push his carriage through the park, tears streaking both your faces, a bleary-eyed family resemblance, and this time everyone will approve and leave you alone, recognizing a good mother who sacrificed sleep for her newborn.

You're aware that these fantasies are not exactly normal. The only person you could explain them to is Lana, but you have the sense to restrain yourself, for if you seem too much alike, she won't see any point in giving her baby up to you.

You talk on the phone with her every week. Thomas is warmed by your commitment to open adoption. Some women would feel threatened. Like your friends at the women's gym where you do the cardio circuit twice a week, who wonder aloud why you don't get a baby from China or Russia, from a family too far away and poor to change their minds. *That's so bourgeois*, you say. A baby doesn't just belong to a couple like a two-door car. Your mother and your aunt raised you, and in a different way, you and Lana will be Maurice's family.

She's heard about your childhood. She confides all sorts of things: Blaine's great talent and half-hearted struggles for sobriety, her attempts to help her ESL students resist the lure of teen pregnancy and street-corner deals. They should aim higher, you agree — you insist. Once, in her lisping, husky voice, she reads you one of her poems. A woman is raped by her lover, and he writes a song about her, or maybe it's only happening in the song, you're not sure. You express sympathy. A mistake. *Not everything is autobiographical.* Over the phone, you hear her frown.

Pauline has been married to her job so long you almost forget that she likes women. She invites you and Thomas to a Friday night cookout at her new girlfriend's house. Beth, a clinic worker at the animal shelter, is tall, ropy, fortyish, with a silvery buzz-cut and Paul Newman eyes. You end up having a lot to say to each other about blues music, your father's one consistent love. One of her housemates strums a guitar, the other flips vegan burgers on the grill. Two spotted dogs with stand-up ears play hide and seek among the crinkly linens hanging from the clothesline on the front lawn. The lemon and lavender dusk is in no hurry to give way to dark. Your sangria recipe is a hit. When you bumble through the house to find the bathroom, you dawdle to look, because doesn't everyone, at what's on the walls and shelves. More CDs than books. The only toys belong to the pets. Their fridge photos are all smiling adults of different ages. You open an art book on the coffee table, close it quickly with a blush. Driving you home, Thomas's only comment is that someday Maurice should have a dog. You pretend to be asleep until you are.

———————

David Copperfield has married a girl who is nothing like his aunt. She is pretty and has no brains. You know from public television that she will die, that this was the only useful thing Charles Dickens could find for her to do.

———————

It is August. Lana gets out of her car. Thomas holds the door open, you take her duffel bag on your shoulder, but the real obstacle to a quick exit from the brown hatchback is the round belly that bows her legs as she eases out into your driveway. The visit's been rescheduled twice because Blaine said he couldn't drive her at the times she was able to go. Finally she's come alone.

Her twiggy body has become pear-shaped. She doesn't resist the drag, the native slowness of her movements now accentuated, so that your first thought of fruit is replaced by one of boats on an invisible current. Though pale, as someone would be who works indoors and at night, her skin has a more nourished look. The drab print smock, the city lipstick, the gap teeth assure you that this is the same Lana who asked two strangers in a coffee shop to help her hold on to her future.

When she leans on you to mount the porch steps, her belly pushes against you, warm and unsettling. She hasn't invited you to feel the baby kick, so you make the most of this touch. You can't know, as she does, what position he's in. He is hidden and close, real and impossible. After your tour of the house, when she gets up to go to the bathroom and you are alone, you sniff the sofa cushion where she — *they* — sat.

Thomas has a list of suggestions for the day: the Mark Twain House, the science museum. None of you have talked about her meeting your friends. Someday, when they've learned what to say. As it turns out, all Lana wants to do is sleep and eat dinner.

The quiet of the house, as she rests and you read, is sad and pleasant. You are absorbed enough to be angry at Steerforth for seducing Little Em'ly, a girl he doesn't need, and to commend yourself on your anger, which you hope to share with Lana, until you consider the triteness of your observations. What do you know about this book, or any book, that she hasn't already learned in high school, turned upside down and ripped apart? What do you know anything about? How to staff a mid-sized office and plant annuals from a hothouse flat. How to marry a man who doesn't look at the sweat-beaded crease between Lana's newly rounded breasts. You have completed the Victorian checklist of success. You could be Agnes, who will receive her reward when all the other characters are out of the way.

Following an easy dinner at a steak and seafood place, Thomas retreats to his home office, and Lana asks to sit with you in the nursery. The loveseat there, with the footstool, is easiest for her back. Comfort wins over any hesitancy about what the room represents. You rush to help her settle. The seat fits you both.

So you're raising him Catholic? she asks.

You've never had that conversation. You don't know what she's thinking. *We're not really anything...but if that's what you want...is it?*

Lana turns toward the white-painted chest of drawers, curtaining her face with her black straight hair. *I just thought, when I saw —*

Thomas's mother must have sent that, you ad-lib. *I guess he put it there for good luck.*

Your gut is certain it's more serious. Over the course of your marriage, Thomas has passed from angry to satirical to conspicuously uninterested in the Jesus news cycle. He wouldn't install an icon out of mere family politeness, like wearing an ugly Christmas sweater from Aunt Sheila.

I didn't think Christianity was about good luck, did you? Lana replies.

There should be somebody pulling the strings, you mean? Making it all come out fairly?

She shifts her weight, considering — *Being able to do the right thing shouldn't depend on what chances you've already had.*

Her head droops. The serenity and fullness shrink away. Tears squeeze out. *Blaine keeps trying to quit,* she insists, *but his chronic pain — and he's had it hard, he grew up in foster homes...* She spreads her hands helplessly over her lap, pushing away the same future for the baby.

Clichés sound false because they're so terribly true. The social worker has taught you what to say when Maurice asks why his real mother didn't want him. *You're doing this out of love,* you tell Lana.

Her gaze is flat. *No. I'm only doing it out of fear.*

You can't not tell her the truth. *Sometimes I feel the same way.*

And then, for the first and only time, she gently takes your hand and holds it against the taut curve of her belly, to feel the fluttering movement beneath.

———————

You buy a doll. Just in case the ultrasound was wrong. And even so, dolls aren't only for little girls. A bald baby with dimpled plastic limbs and a cloth body, no gender. Thomas is reading a book about how to help sons individuate from their mothers. Apparently it will involve a lot of mud and sleeping in the woods. Serves him right. Thomas uses the doll to test whether he can assemble the baby-wearing knapsack without giving its occupant a concussion. You take a lot of cute pictures in those thirty minutes, but he won't let you post them on your Dear Birthmother website.

———————

It is September. A week of silent, crystal-blue mornings. On your front lawn, cut-back spears of iris leaves are streaks of green promise among the perennials' browning husks. Puddles of last night's rain twinkle in the potholes. You finish tucking bulbs into the soil around the big tree, stand and hitch up your gardening jeans, peering up and down the block to see if anyone has noticed you adjusting your underwear in public. The street is empty as usual. Neighbors away for the weekend again, other house still for sale. Not the hardest place to be childless, you once thought. The strip mall with the ice cream parlor, the elementary school playground, are out of earshot on the other side of the subdivision's tree-lined roads. As you survey the newly turned mounds of sun-baked earth, a sharp *crack* echoes in the clear air, sounding like nothing so much as a boy hitting a baseball as far as it could go.

You can't see anything. You decide it doesn't concern you. There's some weeding to be done under the tree, but you'd rather finish planting the rest of the bulbs in the side yard before the sun's too hot. You're halfway down the driveway when it happens. A loud *whoosh*, *crack*, snapping, the crash of a huge shadow across the power lines.

Thomas runs out the front door, mouth agape. *You were right there*, he shouts, grabbing your shoulders, *you were right there*. At first you're annoyed, thinking he's blaming you for not preventing — what?

A tree grows sideways on your lawn. Half a tree. One half standing, as if cleaved by lightning on a cloudless day. The other crushing the bed that you'll have to plant all over again, once the emergency crews have trampled it. A great snagged branch sways from the sagging wire between the telephone poles.

Thomas is pale, sweating and silent. He saw everything from the window while he was shaving. His unfinished stubble ends in a bloody scratch. You love him, but you won't take this the way he does. You weren't dead five minutes ago and you're not dead now. Okay.

Calls are made. The cleanup is coordinated. The tree man explains to Thomas while you're standing there holding his hand.

It was a pear tree. Did you know that?

No.

Fruit trees have to be pruned. This one shouldn't have grown three stories high.

It was like that when we bought the house.

Well. See those brown berries?

The tree man sticks out a leafy branch broken off the tree's canopy. Nubbly fruits like hard, brownish grapes cluster among the leaves.

Those are stunted pears. The treetop got too heavy and it came down.

We didn't know. But half the tree is still good, if we prune it now?

It won't survive the winter with that wound. The trunk's off balance.

Thomas picks a day next month for them to come finish the job. You hope it won't disturb Maurice's nap, but that's none of their business.

In the middle of the night you shock yourself awake, but you'd been doing that anyway, dreaming you got the phone call, or missed it. Thomas is usually up too, shielding the glow of his e-reader under the blanket. You nod at each other and close your eyes.

It is time. You are throwing up. The hospital bathroom is so bare and spotless that you feel guilty being sick in it.

TAKING DOWN THE PEAR TREE   133

You and Thomas have been waiting for two hours in the visitors' lounge of the maternity ward in Springfield. Blaine phoned him this morning to say the baby had been born the night before. Why not sooner? They needed privacy, you tell each other. The cell signal in the hospital is weak. Rooms of sealed air and beige-painted concrete shield the patients temporarily from the world's needs.

You'd stopped hearing from Lana two weeks ago. The last time, she sounded excited about finding a roommate in New York and a night-school teaching gig to tide her over until she started her graduate program in the spring term. You never managed to tell her about the pear tree. Like a lost tooth, you probe for the sensation of death's near-miss and each time find only a gap. She might have helped you find words for this, but you'd been more concerned she would think the house wasn't up to code.

You drove up to Springfield this morning. Thomas activated the reservation at the chain hotel where the three of you — three! — will stay for a few days while the interstate adoption paperwork clears. You unpacked a car-load of diapers, bottles, formula, a suitcase of tiny blue clothes. Baby sold separately.

On your third shaky trip back from the bathroom, Blaine calls Thomas again to say they've already checked out.

Thomas follows Blaine's directions to Lana's apartment, a cement high-rise with a discount supermarket on the ground floor. You edge your way in to a small living room crowded with floor-to-ceiling bookcases. An empty white plastic bassinet on a stand occupies the corner by the door. She'd always said she would want a couple of days to say goodbye to the baby. He'd have to sleep somewhere.

Blaine looks the same: curly-headed boy charmer, worn around the edges. Lana, belly distended in black yoga pants, is topless. On one enlarged reddish-brown nipple she is nursing a white bundle with a striped cap and scrunched-up face.

There he is. He is not fat, beautiful, smiling, like the babies in every adoption advertisement, who naturally must be months older. He does not look like anyone you know or have imagined, except all other newborn white babies. He is a strange new human who has nothing to do with you.

Lana accepts the chocolate box from Thomas while Blaine puts the roses in water to perk up. She is not impolite to you, she still treats you like a friend, asking whether you would like to hold Maurice when he's done feeding. Her contentment is a solid thing. She's in a place beyond words, communicating by touch with the only person who matters.

When you take him in your arms, you don't feel anyone watching you. There is no wrong way to hold him. No part of you that hovers above your head and scolds that your prayers are unconvincing, your love is not enough. You know this at the same time that you know that love is helpless, a leaf clinging to a branch in the flood that sweeps both away.

The baby's eyes are jewel-like blue, his inheritance. Damp black strands peek out from the hospital cap. You brush his peachy cheek with your fingertips, self-conscious that your face and lips are too huge next to his smallness to intrude with a kiss. The books say their eyes can't yet focus to recognize faces, but you're ready to believe every kitschy Irish superstition about the invisible worlds those dark pupils regard. You whisper your name in his ear, and then — *Tell her, tell her...*

Legally, no one can tell Lana what to do. This is her grace period. She will call you. She's tired. The baby, transferred to Thomas's arms, goes back again. Blaine takes him into the bathroom for a fresh diaper. Everyone else goes through the exchange of hugs.

Thomas holds your hand in the elevator. You have learned to recognize his different kinds of quiet: the one where he's sad but doesn't have privacy to show it, the one where he disagrees but it's not the time to speak, the one where he's mad at you but thinks he should wait until he won't lose his temper, by which point you've usually forgotten the incident and resent him dredging it up. Now it is his patient quiet, the tranquility with which he looks at an uncertain future that he still believes could turn up right.

We're never going to see Maurice again, you say. Thomas puts his arm around you. *We don't know that,* he says, secure in his assurance, as you are in your prediction. You hate Lana for making him fallible. He will pray every night till she calls for the last time, and probably several nights thereafter. You won't hear whatever whispered transactions pass between him and the tortured Christ on his plastic rosary, but to you one thing is clear: To know God is to know He can do anything to you without explanation.

It is September. Then it is October. You doze in the daytime between bouts of crying under the red chenille throw on the sofa, wishing your whole day were nothing but the soft light filtered through its warm weave. You are reading *Dombey and Son* because you don't know how it ends. You've watched every episode of a low-budget reality show about aspiring fashion models and you cry along with each girl when she's eliminated for stuttering or falling off her waterskis.

Your co-workers have been kind about your taking the time off that you had planned for maternity leave. Thomas went straight back to work, his way of coping. Everyone has been kind to you in their own inadequate, contradictory ways. Pauline says she never trusted Lana. Your brother, fresh from another girlfriend breakup, touts the unattached lifestyle. Your mother-in-law shares her conviction that everything happens for a reason and God has the perfect baby for you in His own time. You accept it all. You feel imaginary warmth radiating from each sympathy note as you press it to your sore chest, before Thomas comes home and puts them in the box with the others. Dear, stupid words. The perfect ones couldn't have changed anything. You've stopped bothering to get angry that people are lying to you, to themselves. Crying is your pure, single task. The day widens and lengthens to make room for it.

Nevertheless a counter in your head keeps track of the calendar: today Maurice must be a week old, two weeks, a month. Lana must be making arrangements for

TAKING DOWN THE PEAR TREE 137

his care while she's in school this winter. Only, you're guessing she won't go. She'll be a single mother in a ghetto apartment, working a patchwork of day and night jobs, maybe writing poetry in a notebook on long bus rides or maybe giving it up as a youthful affectation. Even now you ache to phone her up, rescue them, beg to make a better family together. But she was always beyond you. Not like you. She had the luxury of choosing to abandon her dreams.

You and Thomas aren't ready to talk about what to do next. Every time you almost ask, you remember watching him from the upstairs window the day you returned from Springfield without Maurice. The tears streamed down his face as he took the empty car seat down to the basement. He never cried in front of you. Some madness had stolen your husband and replaced him with this defeated stranger. Unable to keep looking, you'd caught up the baby doll from the nursery shelf, thinking to hold it for comfort, but found yourself bashing its hard plastic head against the wooden floor till its blinking eyes came loose from their hinges, digging at the seam in its cloth back with your nails to burst the stuffing out. You wailed over the wreck. You might have hidden it from Thomas in the trash, in the past, but you didn't. Covered in one of his silences, he helped you wrap it in a bag in the closet. Since then he hasn't gone into the nursery. You remember to keep the door closed when he's around.

This afternoon, as has become your habit, you sit in the rocking chair from Babies "R" Us and read. The wavering light ripples over the wall as Flora Dombey attends her young brother's deathbed. Moving shadows swoop past your window. You had tuned out the grinding of chainsaws but now you stand and stretch, walk over to watch the men's progress. They have a system of ropes and ladders to fell the branches of the pear tree in a safe order. The last leafy crown is being severed, tipped sideways and lowered onto the pile surrounding the shaved stump. You see for the first time your neighbors' roofs spread out to the wind-polished blue horizon, like *Copperfield*'s ruined Em'ly sighting the coast of Australia, the convicts' promised land, her vineyard of solitude.

An Incomplete List of My Wishes

2017

JENDI REITER

PRIZE WINNER ♦ SHORT STORY COLLECTION

JENDI REITER is the author of the novel *Two Natures* (Saddle Road Press) and four poetry books and chapbooks, most recently *Bullies in Love* (Little Red Tree). Awards include a Massachusetts Cultural Council Fellowship for Poetry, the New Letters Prize for Fiction, the Wag's Revue Poetry Prize, the Bayou Magazine Editor's Prize in Fiction, and two awards from the Poetry Society of America. *Two Natures* won the Rainbow Award for Best Gay Contemporary Fiction and was a finalist for the Book Excellence Awards and the Lascaux Prize for Fiction. Reiter is the editor of WinningWriters.com, an online resource site with contests and markets for creative writers. For literary news, readings, and reviews, visit JendiReiter.com and follow @JendiReiter on Twitter.

BOOKS BY JENDI REITER

Two Natures
SADDLE ROAD PRESS, 2016

Two Natures is the spiritual coming-of-age story of a New York City fashion photographer during the 1990s AIDS crisis.

Named one of Q Spirit's Top LGBTQ Christian Books of 2016, *Two Natures* won the 2016 Rainbow Award for Best Gay Contemporary Fiction and was a finalist for the Lascaux Prize for Fiction, the National Indie Excellence Awards, the Book Excellence Awards, and the American Book Fest Best Book Awards.

"[Julian] brings an outsider's wry and engaging sense of humor to his quest to make it in the New York City fashion world. His romp through gay men's urban culture also holds suffering, grief, pathos, and an ongoing struggle with the God of his childhood, as he comes of age during the height of the AIDS crisis. Though he gets distracted along the way — with politicians, preachers, drag queens, activists, Ironman gym buddies and sex, lots of sex — he never stops looking for real love to redeem him... An entertaining novel and a pleasure to read."

— **Toby Johnson**
Author of *Gay Spirituality* and the novels
Secret Matter and *The Fourth Quill*

"Julian Selkirk gets under our skin. Immediately... Reiter has created a funny, astute, self-deprecating hero, and we care tremendously about what happens to him."

— *A&U: America's AIDS Magazine*

"It's rare to discover within a gay love story an equally powerful undercurrent of political and spiritual examination. Too many gay novels focus on evolving sexuality or love and skim over underlying religious values systems; but one of the special attributes of *Two Natures* isn't just its focus on duality, but its intense revelations about what it means to be both Christian and gay."

— *Midwest Book Review*

Find *Two Natures* at:
bit.ly/two-natures

Read an excerpt at:
bit.ly/two-natures-excerpt

BOOKS BY JENDI REITER

Bullies in Love

LITTLE RED TREE PUBLISHING, 2015

The author's second full-length poetry book includes fine art photography by Massachusetts Cultural Council fellowship winner Toni Pepe. These poems speak of gendered embodiment and its discontents, motherhood after trauma, and finding a spiritual narrative to heal from oppressions both familial and political. Works in this collection won prizes from *Alligator Juniper*, *Atlanta Review*, *Descant*, *New Millennium Writings*, *Solstice Lit Mag*, *Wag's Revue*, and others.

"In this remarkable collection of poems, *Bullies In Love*, Jendi Reiter has created a complex odditorium of characters with unique and often disturbing voices: poems peopled with bullies, the disenfranchised, monsters, prostitutes, criminals, the abused and forgotten, all searching for meaning, for faith and love in a postmodern, often cynical world."

— **Pamela Uschuk**
2010 American Book Award Winner

"Lyric, narrative, prose poem...Jendi Reiter is constantly innovating, injecting the lines with fresh, sharp language and taut, piercing images, which yes, surprise, exhilarate, and delight, but also force the reader to rethink their relationships to social forces. The nature of love and desire are here, but so are family, faith, the body, the natural world, pop culture...even a few stray cats. Jendi explores these as both priestess and stand-up comedian, deploying reverence and humor (sometimes at the same time), and gazing upon whimsy and atrocity with equal scrutiny."

— Charlie Bondhus
Author of *All the Heat We Could Carry*
(Main Street Rag, 2013), 2014 Thom
Gunn Award for Gay Poetry

Find *Bullies in Love* at:
bit.ly/bullies-in-love

Read sample poems at:
bit.ly/bullies-in-love-samples

THE FUTURE IS UP FOR GRABS,
CONCEIVED BY THE IMAGINATION,
CONSTRUCTED WITH WORDS, AND
EXPLAINED AS A STORY.

SUNSHOT 🅢 PRESS

— FIRST PLACE WINNER —
2017 SUNSHOT BOOK AWARD™ FOR FICTION

Bloodshot Stories
by Jeff P. Jones

You want it darker? Jeff P. Jones carries on in the trajectory that runs from Kafka through Philip K. Dick to Cormac McCarthy (with a sprinkling of John Barth thrown in). Whether inviting the reader to comb through the dank stacks of a Stalin archive, or sweat inside the soldered-closed cab of a post-apocalyptic dump truck, or become an atom splitting from the inside, or a single brain dispersing into the universe — these brilliantly researched and deeply imagined stories are never the expected. A stunning collection.

—Janet Burroway

Author of *Writing Fiction: A Guide to Narrative Craft* (9th edition)

SUNSHOT PRESS

— FIRST PLACE WINNER —
2017 SUNSHOT BOOK AWARD™ FOR POETRY

Shot In The Head
by Lee Varon

Lee Varon's poems take us to the shooting of her grandfather in 1936. The images like "a blush that turned to blood," are breath-taking. At first it is a family story, but as you examine it further, the views of prejudice in the community are jaw-dropping, yet amazingly relevant to today's issues. Her grandmother, Virginia Marie, navigates life with pride and loyalty, yet fear and bigotry, highlighting the complexity of human nature.

— Jean Flanagan
Author of *Black Lightning*

SUNSHOT PRESS

2017 SUNSHOT BOOK PRIZE™ FOR NONFICTION

Human Rights and Wrongs
Reluctant Heroes Fight Tyranny
by Adrianne Aron

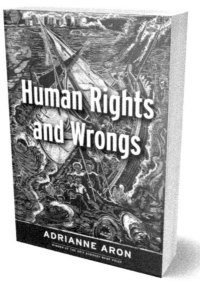

A clever joker once said, 'I dream of a world where chickens can cross the road without having their motives questioned.' I, as a mental health professional, dream of one where psychologists will understand why Ernesto Cruz drinks himself into a stupor, why Eva refuses to speak about what happened to her in Honduras, why Mrs. Malek is afraid to return to Afghanistan. In a collection of serious yet entertaining human interest stories, Adrianne Aron's Human Rights and Wrongs *engages the general reader while inspiring psychologists to think outside the box.*

— Shawn Corne, Ph.D.
Clinical Psychologist, Albany, California

SUNSHOT PRESS

SUNSHOT PRESS WOULD NOT HAVE BEEN POSSIBLE WITHOUT THE BOLD SUPPORT OF THE FOLLOWING POETS & WRITERS:

Barbara A.   Adrianne A.   T. A.   David A.   Idris A.   Kaye A.   Thomas J.   Paul M

Samantha T.   Linda F.   Craig O.   Gary P.   LeeAnn P.   Brian P.   Gary P.   T. M.

Ron V.   Marina H.   Eric W.   Sandra W.   Stuart W.   Emma W.   Fred W.

Rebecca L.   Barbara D.   Dana C.   Elaine C.   Kristen C.   Patricia B.

Timothy W.   James W.   Cynthia W.   Fred W.   Jeanne W.   Lee V.

Benjamin B.   Claire B.   Jerome   Marge B.   Patricia B.   Ruth M.

Barbara S.   Rachel B.   Ellen A.   Patricia R.   Nancy R.   Vincent J.

Alfred M.   Gregory S.   Jan S.   Catherine S.   James S.   Harvey S.

Lisa P.   Luke W.   Leland J.   Gail W.   Lillo W.   Pam W.   Lyzette W.

Terri M.   Sean M.   Deana N.   Jed M.   Barbra N.   Joel N.   Paul N.

Mara S. Ramon B.   Bruce R.   John R.   Jendi R.   Paddy R.   Susan P.

Stanley R.   Andrew S.   Lynn S.   Kathryn P.   Anneliese S.   Mick S.

Lones S.   Corey M.   Richard S.   Nathan S.   Andrew S.   Elaine S.

J.D. B.   Roberta D.   Susan S.   Victoria S.   Joanne S.   Jen S.

Felix N.   Evelyn V.   Derek U.   Mike T.   Naomi M.   Jayshiro T.

Simone M.   Aida Z.   Cindy Z.   Paula Z.   Allan Y.   Felice W.

Tori M.   Karen H.   Ken M.   Barbara M.   Matt M.   Sean M.

Anca H.   David H.   Dennis H.   Eileen H.   Linda H.   W. H.

Kate H.   Jack H.   Roberta H.   Eunice H.   Nancy H.

Jonathan G.   Bruce G.   Joshua B.   Thomas B.   Catherine B.   Enid H.

Susan C.   Danny C.   Laurie C.   Julius C.   Richard B.   R.C. G.   Adam G.

Casey C.   Garry C.   LaRue C.   Bob R.   Kathy C.   Susan C.   Margo B.

Rusty D.   Effie D.   Deborah D.   Annie D.   Howard G.

Bill G.   Tina G.   Nina G.   Paula F.   Jon F.

Jerri B.   Kathryn C.   Robynn C.   Greer G.

William E.   Mary D.   Frank D.   George D.

Ruth F.   Benjamin F.   Teressa E.   Renato E.

Chad F.   Andrew H.   Ann H.   Lorien H.   Jeff J.   Martin I.   Mark H.

Christina F.   Ellen L.   John L.   David L.   Djelloul M.   Bernard M.

Richard L.   Jeffrey M.   Kevin M.   Peter M.   Wendell M.   Clif M.

Genese G.   Howard E.   Alison L.   Kurt L.   Naomi L.   Sam L.

Albert L.   Patricia B.   Chad B.   Mark B.   David B.   Julia L.

Roberta G.   Olaf K.   Kristie L.   Jacqueline L.   Lee L.   Thom K.

Joanne G.   Francis J.   Joyce K.   Marylou S.   Peter K.

James C.   Jason H.   Ryan H.   Georganne H.   Cleda H.

Joan C.   Edie C.

Leslee B.

Beth C.

Jackie M.

THANK YOU

SUNSHOTS.ORG

SUNSHOT S PRESS